720L

17

P9-DMU-736

REVENGE

OF THE FLOWER GIRLS

REVENGE

OF THE FLOWER GIRLS

JENNIFER ZIEGLER

SCHOLASTIC PRESS / NEW YORK

FOR CHRIS

CHAPTER ONE

The Crisis

Darby

It was Delaney's idea that we ruin Lily's wedding. She'll probably argue and say it wasn't, but it was.

We were in an emergency meeting in the Triangular Office — which is our bedroom. We used to have the room next to Lily's, but when we got too big for our cribs, Mom and Dad realized they couldn't fit three beds in there, so they moved us up into the attic. Because our house is old, there are spots that creak when you stand on them and teeny gaps in the wall and floor, but overall it's nice and airy and far away from the other rooms, so we don't have to worry about being heard. It has real wood plank walls and a real wood plank floor and a window that looks out over the front lawn. Not only is it spacious enough for three beds, it also fits three bookcases, three chairs, and a large desk that we share. There's even a big walk-in closet for our clothes, bins of old toys, boxes of Christmas decorations that won't fit in the storage room downstairs, and a collection of wooden Revolutionary War replica swords that Mom only lets us bring out on patriotic holidays.

Anyway, because it's an attic, the ceiling slopes up to a point at the top of the roof like a triangle, so we call it the Triangular Office.

"I call this meeting to order," Dawn said, pounding her fist like a gavel against her headboard. "We need to deal with this very important and horrible situation — which is that our sister is planning to marry a . . . a . . ."

"A rapscallion?" Delaney said.

"A scalawag?" I said.

Dawn considered our suggestions. "I think he's more of a nincompoop."

"Who looks like an armadillo," Delaney added. "Without the shell."

We agreed this was a good comparison. Burton is skinny and squinty-eyed, with a long, thin nose. He never comes out of the library. Plus, he runs funny. We know this because he got scared by a bee a couple of weeks ago.

"What does Lily see in him?" Delaney asked. It was the same question we'd been asking ourselves since she started dating him last December. That's probably why Delaney said it to the piggy bank shaped like the Liberty Bell that she held in her hands. She knew we didn't have any answers.

I should explain that Lily is our older sister. And when I say older, I mean much older. She is twenty-two and we are eleven. After years of being told she couldn't have more babies, our mom was really surprised to find out she was pregnant. She and Dad were even more surprised when they found out she was pregnant with triplets. The family doubled in size in a matter of months. We stayed that way for a long time — Dawn, Delaney, and me, plus Lily, and Mom and Dad — until Mom and Dad divorced two years ago. Now it's just five of us in the house — all girls, unless you count Quincy, our Labrador retriever. But Dad lives just a few minutes away, which means that in addition to our official weekends with him, we often bump into him here and there.

So we all just sat there thinking about how much we loved our sister and how much we disliked the doofus she wanted as her husband. And that's when Delaney said, "We have to stop it."

See? Her idea.

Only . . . we all agreed. We took a vote and every-thing. We just didn't know how we could possibly stop a wedding.

"Darby, you should take notes," Dawn said.

"Me? Why me?"

"As your eldest sister and the future president of the United States, I think we need to put this down on paper so we can figure out what to do."

"Delaney's the youngest, and she's going to be Speaker of the House, where they write the laws," I pointed out. "Shouldn't she do it?"

Dawn shook her head. "You know she can't sit still that long."

"Plus," added Delaney, "you type the fastest."

I did what any person who plans to be chief justice of the United States should do — I listened to all sides before forming my opinion. In this case, I decided they were right. So I sat down at the desk and turned on the computer.

"What are we going to do?" I asked, all ready with my hands on the keyboard.

We sat there for a while, just thinking. Then Dawn said, "Let's review the facts."

So we did. And this is what I typed:

Last Friday, at about 21:00 hours, Lily came home from her date with Burton and called Mom and the three of us into the living room.

Lily was kind of pink-faced and was talking really fast. At first, Mom thought she had been in a car accident, but it was worse than that. She said Burton had asked her to marry him and she said yes.

Mom mumbled, "Oh my."

We mumbled, "Oh no."

Lily told us that they'd decided the wedding would take place in one month. They wanted it to happen soon because once he finishes up a big paper for his master's degree, he's moving to Illinois to go to a law school.

Delaney asked Lily if she would stop studying to be a teacher, and Lily said no — she would just finish her degree in Illinois instead of Texas.

I asked her if she and Burton would get married on the hill. (The hill is on our property behind our house. It's great for the Slip 'N Slide. Lily loves it, too, and she always said she wanted to get married on it, right at sunset.)

Lily said no. Burton has allergies.

She then said that we would be in the wedding, too. Dawn asked who we were going to marry, and Lily said no one. We were going to be her flower girls.

Only, she said we wouldn't scatter real flowers. We would have to use fake ones. Because Burton has allergies.

Mom mumbled, "Oh boy."

We mumbled, "Oh no." (Actually, it was a little louder than a mumble.)

Delaney pointed out that this would make us "fake flower girls," and Dawn and I agreed. Lily just laughed and said that we would be real flower girls — even if the flowers were plastic.

Then Lily said, "I better call Dad," and went into Mom's office.

We turned toward Mom and started saying things like "Isn't it horrible?" and "Plastic flowers are stupid" and "Tell her she can't do it!"

Mom said that Lily was a grown woman and could make her own decisions. She said we needed to give Burton a chance, and that the main reason we don't like him is because we miss Alex.

Then Mom said she had a headache and went to lie down.

"Mom's right," Dawn said, reading over my shoulder. "I miss Alex."

"Me, too," I said.

"Me three," Delaney said.

Alex was Lily's boyfriend before Burton. They met in middle school and started to date their sophomore year of high school. He used to hang out here with her all the time. His favorite president is Thomas Jefferson. We all respect that.

Once, Dawn asked Burton who his favorite U.S. president was, and do you know what he said? Franklin Pierce! We asked why, and he said because he was President Pierce's great-great-great-grandnephew — or something like that. Now, the three of us don't even agree on who the best president was. Dawn's favorite is Washington, Delaney's is Lincoln, and mine is Franklin Delano Roosevelt. But we all agree that they were good ones. And we all agree that Pierce was *not* one of the best.

Anyway, when Lily and Alex graduated high school, Lily went to the University of Texas just down the road in Austin, and Alex went to Tulane University in New Orleans. They were still a couple, though, and Alex would visit during the breaks and occasionally on a weekend. But for some reason, they broke up last summer. Lily never said why — she just went all mopey and droopy-looking for a long time. And then Burton nosed his way into her life.

For the rest of the meeting — in fact, for the rest of the weekend — we were too sad to think of ideas. It started to seem like we were going to end up related to a sneezy, squinty, Franklin Pierce–loving armadillo.

Then, on Monday, Delaney saw Alex downtown and everything changed. . . .

CHAPTER TWO

Negotiations

Delaney

It's true I said we should stop the wedding from happening, but I didn't mean we should ruin it. I was thinking we could come up with a way to talk Lily out of it. My sisters will say that I never stop talking. Dawn is all about decision making, and Darby is all about thinking and dreaming, but I like to discuss things.

Only, I couldn't figure out what to say to Lily. I couldn't exactly tell her that we hated her fiancé because he liked the nincompoopiest of all presidents. Or because he looked like he should be digging a burrow somewhere out in the Hill Country. Or because he wasn't Alex.

The thing was, Alex just looked better with Lily. Not because he was handsomer, which we all thought he was. It was just that, whenever she was with him, Lily was all shiny and bright and laughed a lot. Burton never made her laugh. He never booped the end of her nose when she looked worried. And he never brought her things that he found on his walks — like wildflowers or clam fossils shaped like hearts. (Burton doesn't take walks. Because Burton has allergies.)

But when we said all these things to Mom, she said we were being silly. And once, when we asked Burton why he never picked wildflowers for Lily, he said it was illegal — and they made him sneeze. All the things we thought were important didn't seem to matter to anyone else.

Then Mom decided to invite Burton and his mother over for dinner Monday night. And anytime we have company over, Mom makes a peach cobbler. That morning, she discovered she needed a new can of shortening in order to make it. I was the only triplet in sight when she made this realization, so she sent me down to Ever's Corner Store.

Ever's is this old-timey place that was built back when Eisenhower was president. The coolest part about the store is the soda fountain, so folks mainly go in there for the homemade shakes and burgers, and they hardly ever shop. Because of this, a lot of the stuff on their shelves is dusty or expired, and we all call it Forever's. Our neighbor, Ms. Woolcott, once bought a box of panty hose and found a mouse living in it. We could hear her scream as we ate our breakfast.

Anyway, so there I was in Forever's, wiping off a can with the end of my shirt to see if it might be shortening, when I saw someone familiar walk away from the front counter.

Alex!

"Alex! Alex! Alex!" I started yelling, and jumping up and down as if I were barefoot on hot pavement.

"Hey, Delaney," he said, swerving to meet up with me. Unlike Burton, who was always calling us Debbie or Dana or Delilah, Alex never got us confused. Also, unlike Burton, Alex doesn't resemble any funny-looking critters. He's handsome the same way Lily is pretty — in a friendly, natural sort of way. His eyes are big and round like hers, but dark brown instead of blue. And he smiles and laughs a lot, just like Lily. (The way she used to anyhow.)

"What are you doing here?" I asked him, still hopping a little.

"Just had a root beer float."

"No. I mean, how come you're in Texas?"

"I'm home for the summer and interning as a clerk in the courthouse. Was just on my lunch break," he said.

Seeing him filled me with warm, cozy, familiar feelings. Then I felt sad, because I remembered that we never got to see him on purpose anymore — only on accident.

"You know what? You should come by the house," I said. "How about tomorrow? Lily got us cookie cutters in the shape of Lincoln's head. We could make chocolate chip."

Alex's smile slowly drooped. "Ah . . . um . . . maybe," he said.

"Don't do that, Alex," I said. "Don't be one of those grown-ups who say 'maybe' when they mean 'no.'"

He chuckled. "You girls are smarter than most college students."

"Oh, come on. Please? You could see Dawn and Darby and Mom and Quincy. And you could see Lily."

"That's just it," he said with a sigh. "Lily and I haven't talked in a long while. I'm not sure she'd appreciate my showing up out of the blue."

"I bet she would."

Alex's eyes got big. "Think so? But isn't she still seeing what's-his-name?"

"Burton?" I could feel my face bunch up, as if I were smelling something bad. "It's worse than you know. Not only is she still seeing him, they're getting married in three and a half weeks."

"They're *what*?" Alex stared past me at a display of diapers. I thought maybe he saw a mouse or something, because his mouth was all frowny and his face went kind of pale. But when I turned my head to check, everything looked all right.

That's when I realized what his expression was for: He was upset to hear the news. Which meant that he still liked Lily!

"Come on, Alex," I said, all whiny and pleading. "Please come out and visit."

"I really don't think I should." His voice was quieter than it was before. "Sorry, Delaney. I'd love to, but your sister is moving on. I have to respect that."

"But you still care about her, right? You guys can still be friends, right?"

"Well . . . yeah, but —"

"And friends visit each other, right?"

"Sure they do, but —"

"Then come visit!"

Alex shook his head. "Maybe someday," he said. "If she were to invite me, I'd know it was okay to do things like that — to be friends. But she hasn't. I really appreciate the invitation, and I'd really like to see all of you, but unless Lily reaches out, I have to assume she doesn't want me around."

"But . . . but . . ." I sounded all sputtery — like Dad's Vespa. I just couldn't think of anything else to say.

Alex patted me on the shoulder. "I've got to run, but I'm so glad I saw you. Please tell your family hi from me, okay?" Before I could say anything back to him, he turned and walked out.

I was bummed to see him leave, but then a huge smile popped out on my face.

Because, suddenly, I knew exactly what we needed to do.

CHAPTER THREE

Conference

Dawn

While Delaney was out talking with Alex, I was in the Triangular Office, reading a book on Lyndon Baines Johnson. Even though we're mad at him for picking up his beagle by the ears, Darby, Delaney, and I still think he is one of the most underappreciated presidents. Plus our town, Johnson City, was named for his family, which sort of makes him our neighbor. At some point, I got thirsty and went downstairs.

The door to the attic is at the end of the hall, near Mom's bathroom. Mom's shower makes creepy groaning noises, even when it isn't running — as if there's a ghost. Sometimes, when I'm going up or down the stairs by myself, I get scared and run past that part of the house — just in case something might want to jump out and grab me. Delaney does this, too. Darby isn't scared, but not because she doesn't think there's a ghost — she does. She just thinks ghosts can't hurt us. Me? I'd rather be safe than sorry.

Anyway, so there I was, headed to the kitchen for a juice box. I did a speedy walk past Mom's bathroom and was just slowing down when, out of the corner of my eye, I saw something big and white and fluttery in Lily's room. *The ghost!*

You'd think I would have screamed. Or run. Or called for help. Right? Nope. I froze.

I stood on my left foot, my right foot stretched behind me, as if I were a statue of a walking girl. Only, I couldn't move. I just kept staring at the big white thing that flapped and wavered and rustled in front of me. Then the white thing started making little grunting sounds. I could feel a scream start to come up my throat and then . . . Lily's head suddenly popped out of the white thing!

"*Aaaaaaaaaaaaaaaaaah!*" I yelled, still too scared to move.

"*Aaaaaaaaaaaaaaaaaah!*" went Lily's head. Then her head looked kind of mad at me and said, "What are you doing?"

And that's when I noticed the white thing wasn't a ghost. Lily was wearing a gigantic white dress. The skirt part was so big she probably couldn't fit through the doorway. And at the tops of the sleeves were big, poufy things that stuck up like giant marshmallows.

"Why are you yelling, Dawn?" she asked. She walked over to the doorway, her dress making loud swishy sounds.

"What are you wearing?" I asked.

A funny look came over Lily's face. "It's, um . . . it's a wedding dress. It used to belong to Burton's mom. She wants me to wear it at the wedding."

"All of it?" I asked, patting the skirt. It felt like twelve skirts on top of one another underneath.

She smiled a tiny smile. "Yes, all of it."

"But it's ugly."

Lily turned and looked at herself in the mirror over her dresser. "It's not that bad," she said. Only, she seemed to be saying it to her reflection, not to me. And judging by the squiggly lines on her forehead, her reflection didn't believe it.

I walked into her room and sat down on her bed, watching her as she turned this way and that, studying herself.

"It's so big and ugly, I thought you were a ghost," I said. "That's why I screamed."

Lily laughed a little. "Are you guys still scared of Mom's bathroom? You know those sounds are just air trapped in the old pipes, right?" She sat down next to me on the bed, and her skirt puffed up real high. She tried to pat it down with her hands, but that didn't make much difference.

I didn't answer her. I was feeling sad and scared. Not the kind of scared like I was of the ghost — I mean the kind of twisted-up feelings you get when you know things are changing and you don't want them to.

"Why aren't you with Alex anymore?" I didn't realize I was going to ask her that. The words just sort of burst out of my mouth.

Lily's face went cloudy and hard to read — like when the screen saver comes on the computer monitor. "People change after high school," she said. She turned her head and stared out the window toward the hill. I couldn't see her eyes, but her voice sounded sad. Her voice sounded sad a lot this past year. "They want to do new things, go to new places, make new friends. They leave high school things — and high school people — behind."

"Are you saying that you changed or that Alex changed?" I asked.

She was quiet for a few seconds. "I guess we both did."

I stared at her. She looked so silly in the dress, but she was still beautiful. It's perfect that her name is Lily. She really is a lot like a flower. She likes to be out in the sun and fresh air. She's sweet and happy and makes everything better just by being there. At least, she used to be. Ever since last Christmas, she'd been quieter and less smiley. And her forehead almost always had those wavy lines.

A new scary thought popped into my mind. "Are me, Darby, and Delaney going to have to wear big ghost dresses at the wedding, too?"

Lily laughed. "No way," she said. "No ghost dresses. I promise."

"Really?" This made me feel so much better. Lily always wears pretty dresses (the simple cottony kind, not like Burton's mother's dress), and her hair is long and flowy. But Darby, Delaney, and I prefer shorts or jeans. And even though we have long brownish-blondish hair like Lily's, we always put it in braids. If they made each of us wear a monster dress with seven skirts, and sleeves that pouf up like balloons, we probably wouldn't know how to move. They'd have to wheel us down the aisle.

"It's not fair that you don't get your own dress," I said. "This one is so . . . not Lily-like."

"I know, but it means a lot to Burton's mom. Besides, he and I don't have a lot of money, and this way we don't have to buy the dress or the ring."

My eyes got big. "She's giving you a ring, too?"

"Yep. I haven't been wearing it because it needs to be resized." Lily reached into the drawer on her bedside table and pulled out a small velvet-covered box. She flipped open the top, and inside was the most awful-looking ring I've ever seen. It was even worse than the dress.

"I don't get it. Why does it have a letter *U*?" I pointed to the stones in a smushed semicircle shape.

"It's a horseshoe," she said. "For luck."

It didn't look like a horseshoe. I didn't want to say it — but it looked like a toilet seat.

"How can that ring be lucky?" I asked. "I thought you said his parents are divorced, just like Mom and Dad."

"Well . . . it's lucky because we don't have to pay for it," she said, with a nervous-sounding laugh. "I think his mom is just trying to help."

"Or she's trying to make you turn into her," I grumbled. The sad, twisty feelings were turning into anger. "You aren't going to get married on the hill, even though you always wanted to. You aren't going to have flowers, even though you love them, because Burton gets sneezy. You have to wear a big scary dress and old weird ring and basically not do anything you want to do on your wedding day. Am I right?"

Lily tucked a piece of my hair behind my ear. "You don't understand," she said. "When you love someone, you are willing to give up things that you once thought were important to you."

"Okay. I see *you* doing that. But is Burton doing that, too?"

She stared down at the ring on her finger, and the squiggles came back to her forehead. Then she turned to face me. "You're young," she said. "You just can't understand. Not until you're older."

Lily never said stuff like that. Lots of grown-ups do, but not her. Only . . . Lily was doing lots of things now I never thought she would. And she wasn't doing the things she used to always do.

I wanted things to go back to the way they were. I wanted old Lily, not new Lily. I wanted the Lily who would come into our rooms to play Presidential Trivia and watch us do reenactments. The Lily who read every single Harry Potter book aloud to us — making different voices for the characters and everything. The Lily who would pick wildflowers on the hill and cry every time we watched the Toy Story movies together. The

Lily who loved animals so much, she stopped eating meat when she was twelve years old. The Lily who smiled and laughed all the time and gave the world's best hugs.

It was weird, but even though she was sitting right next to me, I was really missing her.

CHAPTER FOUR

Home Front

Darby

We had run the sprinklers that morning, and our dog, Quincy, loves to go find mud and roll in it. But since Mom didn't want the house getting all dirty, with Burton and his mother coming to visit, she put Quincy in his kennel on the front porch until the yard dried out. This always makes me feel bad for him, so I decided to keep him company — even though he mainly just lay there and snored.

I was stretched out along the porch swing, enjoying the songs of nearby mockingbirds and the *whoosh* of traffic on Highway 290 a couple of miles away and the snorts and whistles of Quincy's heavy sleep. I'm the only triplet who can just sit and do nothing. Dawn is always in the middle of some important project, and Delaney has to be bouncing around and talking a mile a minute — even if bugs or a sacked-out dog are the only ones around to listen.

Then I heard what I first thought was a funny-sounding bird.

"Yoo-hoo! Hello there! Yoo-hoo!"

I sat up and glanced about. Ms. Woolcott was standing by the low, wooden crisscross fence that separates our property from hers. As usual, her hair was heavily sprayed and stood up high on her head like a dandelion gone to seed. She was wearing her gardening gloves and clogs and waved a pair of pruning shears as she called out to me. Ms. Woolcott always seems to be dressed up. Even when she's doing yard work, she wears wide colorful skirts that really stand out and that Dad says he wishes were four inches longer. Today, her skirt was bright pink with embroidered curlicue daisies growing up from the bottom seam.

I glanced down at Quincy, but he had long ago learned to ignore Ms. Woolcott. I thought about ignoring her, too — of all us triplets, I'm the shyest — but I figured that wouldn't be neighborly. So I got up and walked to the fence.

"Good morning, Ms. Woolcott," I said.

"Good morning, Delaney," she said. Or sang. Ms.

Woolcott always sings her words instead of just saying them.

"I'm Darby," I corrected. "Delaney went to Forev — I
mean, Ever's store to get some shortening for Mom's
cobbler."

At my mention of Ever's, a funny look came over Ms.
Woolcott's face, and she seemed to shudder a bit. Soon,
it passed and she smiled real big.

"Her peach cobbler? Oh? Sounds as if there's a special
occasion coming up. Hmm?"

It was my turn to shudder a little. That sentence was
like part of an opera.

Ms. Woolcott's first name is Josephine and she goes
by Josie with other adults, but I've heard Mom call her
Nosy Josie when she thinks we aren't listening. Ms.
Woolcott is nice, but she really does try to make everybody's business her own.

"Sort of," I said. "See, Lily is getting married —"

At this, Ms. Woolcott gasped really huge and loud.

" — to Burton Caldwell, so we invited him and his
mom over to dinner to get to know them better."

All the air suddenly popped out of Ms. Woolcott, and
her shoulders slumped — as if she were a punctured
beach ball. "She's marrying Burton Caldwell?" she
asked, her face as droopy as her shoulders. "You mean

the Caldwells who tried to get the city to remove all the flowering trees on Main Street? Are you sure that's the one?"

I wanted to tell her that I was darn well sure about who my sister was marrying — and if I had been Dawn, I probably would have (Dawn has a temper). Instead, I said, "'Fraid so."

"But . . . what about Alex?"

"They broke up last year. Then she started dating Burton. Now they're getting married."

"Oh no! I'm so sorry to hear that! What a shame."

I tilted my head. "Do you mean it's a shame that she's getting married to Burton or that she and Alex broke up?"

Ms. Woolcott's cheeks turned as pink as her skirt. "Oh, well . . . of course, I didn't mean to imply . . . Weddings are always a blessing, right? . . . As long as she's happy." She smiled and nodded.

"I guess."

Ms. Woolcott looked over at our house. Her smile faded and her nodding turned into a head shake. "It's just that . . . Lily and Alex made the perfect couple. Ab-so-LUTE-ly perfect."

It was true. Lily and Alex just seemed to belong together, and it seemed wrong that they would break up. It's like when you try to have strawberry shortcake without whipped cream. It's still good, but you can't help thinking that something important is missing, something that just makes it better.

With Alex, Lily was better. She was happier. She was Lily-er.

Ms. Woolcott was still shaking her head sadly. I was thinking how nice it was for her to also be worried about Lily. Then I started thinking about her hair and how incredible it was that neither the breeze nor her movements could jostle it.

"Well, do tell your family I said hello," Ms. Woolcott trilled. She turned and started walking back toward her house. After a few steps, I could hear her say "ab-so-LUTE-ly perfect" again.

I went back to the porch and tried to relax and daydream again, but everything was different now. For one thing, I'd started fretting about Burton and Lily. And also, the sounds were all different. The birds had stopped singing, and I could hear angry voices coming from inside the house.

"Mom, *please*!" Lily was saying.

"No," Mom replied. "And please do not bring it up again."

Quincy wasn't asleep anymore either. Now he was fidgety and whimpering.

Just then, the front door slowly opened, and Dawn slipped out onto the porch. She sat down next to me on the swing, her face puckered with worry.

"What's going on?" I asked.

"Lily wants Dad to come to the dinner for Burton and his mother, but Mom's being stubborn."

We both sighed and glanced down at our bare feet. Mom and Dad don't say bad things about each other, but they also don't talk to each other much. We hate this more than anything in the world — more than Burton even.

"Burton's father isn't going to be there, so why should yours?" we heard Mom say.

"Burton's dad is in South America. He can't simply fly up for peach cobbler!"

My toes and Dawn's toes pushed against the wooden floor planks simultaneously and we started the swing rocking. We didn't decide ahead of time, we just did it — at the exact same second. Things like that happen when you're a triplet.

The back-and-forth motion of the swing made me feel a little better, and probably soothed Dawn, too. Also the creaking sounds drowned out the angry talk.

"What's going on?"

Delaney was coming up the path, holding a cloth

grocery sack. She could tell right away that something was up. Like I said, it's a triplet thing. Or at least a sister thing.

As she came up the steps, we told her about Lily and Mom arguing about Dad. She looked sad for a moment, and then all of a sudden, she got big-eyed and bouncy.

"Guess who I saw at Forever's!" Before we could guess, she said, "Alex! Alex, Alex, Alex!"

Dawn and I traded surprised looks.

"He's in town?" I asked.

"Lucky!" said Dawn. "I want to see him."

"He's in town for the summer and" — Delaney paused and bounced some more — "he's still in love with Lily!"

"He said that?" I asked.

"Well . . . no, but I could tell."

"Hey, wait," said Dawn. "I talked with Lily just now, and I think she still loves Alex, too."

"Even Ms. Woolcott can't believe they broke up," I said. "But what difference does all this make if Lily's set on marrying Burton?"

Delaney raised her hand. "I know! I know! I know what we need to do!"

"What?" Dawn and I said together.

"We have to get Lily and Alex together. Once they see each other, they'll realize they shouldn't have broken up!"

We all agreed that Delaney's plan was a good one, but we couldn't figure out how to do that. Delaney said she'd tried to invite him over, but he would come only if Lily did the asking.

"We better work out something fast," I pointed out, "before she gets all busy with the wedding."

The three of us put our hands together. Delaney first, then mine on top of hers, and then Dawn's on top. Then we all repeated after Dawn.

"I, Dawn Brewster" — only, we all said our own name — "do solemnly swear that we will do everything in our power to get Lily reunited with Alex in some way . . . and we will continue in our efforts to stop her marriage to Burton . . . with the flag of our fathers —" She nodded toward the American flag that hung limply on our flagpole in the front yard.

"And mothers," I added.

"And mothers," Dawn repeated, "as witness, and with all the power and freedom of the republic it stands for . . . and with our loyal hound as witness . . ."

"Get on with it!" Delaney whined, bouncing on her toes.

"We hereby swear . . . with justice for all . . . amen . . . over and out."

"Well, that's dandy," I said, sitting back down on the swing. "Now we just need to come up with our next move."

My sisters sat down on either side of me, and all three of us started pushing the swing at the same time. No one said a word as we tried to think of a plan.

After a while, the front door opened and Lily came onto the porch.

"Hey, gang. Guess what! I have big news," she said.

"The wedding is canceled?" Delaney asked.

Lily gave her a funny look. "No. No, of course not." She clapped her hands together and smiled a huge smile. "Dad will be joining us for supper!"

"Wow," I said, feeling my eyes pop a little. That really was big news. Lily must have actually won an argument with Mom — and that never happens.

"Just think," Lily said dreamily. "All of the most important people in my life will be here, eating at the same table."

She turned and stepped back into the house, closing the door behind her.

"Not *all* the important people," Delaney muttered.

"Yeah. The president is important and he isn't coming," Dawn said.

"I meant Alex!" Delaney said in a whiny voice.

Dawn nodded. "Right. Him, too."

The three of us pushed our feet against the porch planks and together we resumed swinging and pondering.

CHAPTER FIVE

Peace Offerings

Delaney

Burton's mother doesn't look like an armadillo. She has the same pointy nose as Burton's, but otherwise she's as wide-eyed and twitchy as a deer. Darby keeps saying she's more like a scared rabbit, but that's wrong. Rabbits are soft, and there's a toughness about Mrs. Caldwell. She may spook easily, but she'd probably kick you before she ran off.

Mom usually runs late when she cooks. Sure enough, by the time Mrs. Caldwell rang the doorbell, Mom was busy in the kitchen with three pots on the stove and something in the oven and had already sent Lily and Burton to the store for ice cream to go with the cobbler. That left the three of us to let Burton's mom in. Since none of us wanted to answer the bell, we decided to all do it together. We put our hands on the doorknob, turned it, and slowly passed the door along to one another as we opened it wide.

Mrs. Caldwell seemed startled at the sight of all three of us. Instead of saying hi, she said, "Oh, that's right. Burton said there were triplets."

"Welcome," Dawn said in her best grown-up voice. "Won't you please come in?"

As Mrs. Caldwell stepped inside, her eyes darted all around, as if she expected to see six more of us standing about the room. Dawn stepped forward and offered to take the package she was holding, but Mrs. Caldwell almost didn't want to give it to her. "Do be careful," she said as Dawn took it from her hands. "It's a hostess gift for your mother. It's not a toy. It's breakable. Please do be gentle with that." I could see Dawn stiffen up with anger. Darby and I traded worried looks. We could tell Dawn was considering dropping the package on purpose. Or maybe tossing it at Mrs. Caldwell's head.

Luckily, Mom walked into the room right at that point. "Hello, I'm Annie," she said in the soft, gentle voice she uses with her clients. She took the gift and thanked Mrs. Caldwell. "Won't you have a seat?" she said, gesturing toward the couch and armchairs.

But before Mrs. Caldwell could sit down, the front door opened beside her, making her jump. Daddy's head poked in, saying, "Knock, knock!"

Dawn, Darby, and I were so happy to see him, we literally jumped up and down and squealed. Even Quincy ran circles around him, wagging his tail. Dad alternated among the three of us, throwing us over his shoulder and spinning us. The whole time, Mrs. Caldwell pressed herself against the wall, wincing and saying things like "Oh! Oh my! Watch out now!"

Then Darby begged Dad to do the grizzly bear. When he let out his fierce "*Rowr!*" and chased Darby down the hall, I thought Mrs. Caldwell was going to tear out the door and run to the next county.

Instead, she just stood there, flinching every time Darby let out a scream. At one point, she turned to Mom and said, "Shouldn't you stop it? Aren't you worried something might happen?"

Mom, who at first didn't look all that thrilled to see Dad, lifted her chin the way she does when someone has made her mad. "No, of course I'm not worried," Mom said. Her smile seemed all wrong — as if she wasn't the one making it, and instead, invisible fingers were yanking the corners of her mouth.

"But what if something gets broken?" Mrs. Caldwell

said, glancing nervously toward the sound of Dad's *rowr* sounds.

"I can assure you, everything's fine. I know it's rambunctious, but nothing has ever gone wrong."

"Except for that time when Darby peed her pants," I reminded Mom.

Mom gave me a funny look. "Yes, Delaney. Except for that one time."

"It looks crazy, but it's what dads do," Dawn said in her I-know-everything voice.

"Not Burton's dad." Mrs. Caldwell shook her head vigorously. "Burton is brilliant, as you know, so I wouldn't allow such things. Horseplay like that might damage the brain."

Again, the invisible fingers stretched Mom's mouth tightly. "Don't worry yourself, Mrs. Caldwell. I'm sure Darby is fine."

At that point, Dad came back into the room with Darby tossed over his shoulder. She was giggling and hiccupping and her face was the color of a fire truck. Dad set her down and stepped forward to shake Mrs. Caldwell's hand. "Hi there," he said, a little out of breath. "You must be Mrs. Caldwell. I'm Phil Brewster."

"Hi. Please call me Edith."

They shook hands and nodded, and then the grown-ups just kind of stood there, smiling at one another. It felt weird — especially after the noise of Daddy's arrival. Then they all started to talk at once, and then they all laughed. Then everything got quiet again. And that's when Lily and Burton walked in. Burton looked as he always did, with his leather briefcase pressed up against him as if he were hugging it. Lily carried a grocery sack.

Everyone seemed incredibly happy to see them, as if they'd been gone for years. After they finished all the greetings, Mom turned to me, Dawn, and Darby, and told us to go upstairs until it was time to eat.

In a way, I didn't want to go, because we were supposed to be gathering intelligence for Operation Stop-the-Wedding. But I was glad, too, because things felt so nervous and icky downstairs. Even Quincy had run off somewhere to hide. Also, if we stayed, we'd probably have to sit in a chair and be quiet for a long time, and that's hard for me.

As soon as we got up to the Triangular Office, Dawn started complaining.

"Did you hear her? Mrs. Caldwell thinks we're ruffians."

Darby nodded. "Hooligans."

"Yep," I agreed. "She thinks our whole house is full of untamed goons. She was probably afraid we'd bite her."

"I wanted to," grumbled Dawn.

"Just think," I said. "If Lily marries Burton, she'll come over more often."

"Unless I bite her," Dawn said.

"Well, let's face it. We weren't going to like her, no matter what," Darby pointed out. Darby has a talent for shutting us down when we grumble and whine. It's really frustrating.

"Girls?" Lily walked into our room, still carrying the grocery bag. "Can I come in?"

"Of course!" I said. "What are you doing up here? Is it really bad downstairs? Did Mrs. Caldwell get mad and leave?"

Lily chuckled a little bit. "No, it's fine. In fact, I'm really proud of Mom and Dad. They are on their best behavior."

"That's a good thing about tonight," Darby said. "It's great to see Dad here for more than five minutes. And he played grizzly bear!"

Darby always loved Daddy's grizzly bear game. They hardly ever play it now, though. Dad's apartment has only four small rooms, so it isn't much fun there.

"I came up for a couple of reasons," Lily said. She crossed the room and sat down on Dawn's bed — probably because it was the only one that was made. "First of all, Mom wants you to wash up because dinner will be served very soon. And second, I come bearing gifts."

"Gifts?" we all said at the same time.

"Yes," she said. "For you."

"Aww . . . you didn't have to do that," Darby said.

"I didn't." Lily tried to smile, but it looked like that finger-pulling-lips face Mom had made. "Burton did."

"Burton?" we said at the same time.

"He saw this and thought you should have it." She pulled out a parcel that had been wrapped in a brown paper bag and stapled shut. "You'll have to share," she explained.

Dawn, Darby, and I glanced at each other, unsure what to think. What do you do when the enemy gives you a present?

Eventually, Dawn tore open the paper. Inside was a rectangular box containing a set of three plastic glittery cats. Sparkle Cats. They all come in colors like green, blue, pink, and purple and have names like Toodle Lou and Giggle Pod and Bubble-kins. Some of our friends at school were into them three years ago. We never were. While we played Presidential Trivia and tried to hold quidditch matches, other girls were running around the playground meowing and pretending to lick their paws and casting "sparkle spells."

"What are we supposed to do with these?" Dawn asked Lily.

Lily sighed. "Look, I know it's not exactly your thing, but he saw it at the store and wanted to get it for you three. He's trying."

I picked up the box. "'Glow-in-the-dark with motion-sensor purring sounds,'" I read aloud. "That could be . . . cool. I guess."

"See?" Lily said. "And it's the thought that counts. He wanted to do something nice for you three. After he gets to know you better, he'll be able to choose gifts that are more to your liking."

I wanted to point something out, but I didn't. I wanted to say that there were other things on the box. Like the words FOR AGES 3 TO 8 and a bright orange circular sticker that read CLEARANCE. But I didn't. Lily seemed happy that Burton was trying to make us happy, so it seemed wrong to grumble about it.

"I know you aren't big fans of Burton, but that's because you don't know him that well yet," she said. "Promise me you'll be nice to him tonight — okay?"

We mumbled our promises.

Lily smiled. "Thanks. Now please wash up and come into the dining room to eat," she said as she headed out of our room.

After her footsteps faded away, Dawn said, "Great googly moogly. That is the lousiest present I ever saw."

"Is it right to hate a gift when you weren't even expecting one?" Darby asked. "I mean, it isn't our birthday or Christmas or anything."

I shrugged. "I don't know. But I do know that Alex would never have bought us something like that."

As we tramped down the steps to go wash up and eat, I felt kind of heavy and slow. Everyone seemed to be pretending to feel things they weren't feeling, or to like someone they didn't like, or to be thankful for something they really didn't appreciate.

The whole world was upside down and backward and you never knew what to expect. It was sort of like Dad's grizzly bear game — only, not fun at all.

CHAPTER SIX

State Dinner

Dawn

The best part about dinner was having Dad there — our whole family eating at the same table for the first time in two years. Also, Mom's peach cobbler was delectable. Other than that, everything was a disaster.

We ate in the formal dining room — also something we hadn't done since Dad left and Lily went off to college. I sat in the middle of one side of the long pine table with Darby and Delaney. Across from me sat Burton, with his mom and Lily on either side of him. Mom and Dad sat on the two ends, as far away from each other as possible.

All through the salad, Mrs. Caldwell kept talking about Burton. Did you know he cured cancer, won ten Olympic gold medals, and earned three Nobel Prizes all while battling ogres, and he never once forgot to wipe his feet before stepping indoors? Well, he didn't do any of those things. But you'd think he had, the way his mom kept yammering on.

Burton didn't seem to enjoy it either. While she jabbered about his genius, he just ducked his head and kept rearranging his salad. And his ears turned the same color as the cherry tomatoes. The only time he really talked was during the main course, when Daddy asked him about his studies. Burton went on and on about research methodology and his acceptance to law school in Chicago.

"Lots of U.S. presidents have started out as lawyers," Delaney said. She's always butting into conversations. It's like her superpower.

"Yes," Burton said. "I suppose that's right."

"It *is* right," I said. Mom gave me a warning look.

"Have you ever thought about running for office?" Delaney asked Burton.

Burton did his laugh-that-doesn't-seem-like-a-laugh. It's when he smiles and lets out air really fast. More of a pant, really. "No," he said. "I'm afraid I'm just too busy for stuff like that."

I hated the way he said "stuff like that" and waved his hand as if he were dismissing someone offering him dessert. Serving in government is a noble thing to do, and he was acting like it was junk food.

"Well, good for you for knowing yourself," Daddy said. He and Darby are always trying to see the positive side of people — both friend and foe. It's kind of annoying.

"Politics isn't for everyone," Daddy went on. "Heck, even most people who do it aren't that good at it."

"He would be good at it," Mrs. Caldwell said. "You should at least think about it, Burton dear. You'd make an excellent . . . whatever it is you run for."

"President?" Delaney asked.

"Yes. Why not?" Mrs. Caldwell said. "He'd certainly be better than this . . . simpleton we have now."

I think I made a slight growling noise, because Darby and Delaney both looked at me. No one else seemed to hear it, though. I stared down at my chicken and dumplings. Even if I hadn't lost my appetite, I couldn't have eaten anymore. My molars were clamped so tightly, it was like they were Super Glued together.

No matter what — even if you don't agree with the person doing the job — you have to respect the office of the presidency. I wanted to say that (or holler that) to Mrs. Caldwell, but Darby was squeezing my arm under the table. I knew it was her way of reminding me about our promise to Lily.

"So, Burton," Delaney said kind of loudly — I guess to cover up any more growling noises. "Who did you vote for in the last election?"

He made another one of those waves, as if pushing away her words, and said, "Nobody. I didn't have time for that."

The next thing I knew, my fork dropped onto my plate with a loud *clang*, and I was jumping to my feet. Darby and Delaney disagree on what they saw. According to Delaney, I clearly said, "Let me at him," and leaned forward as if I were going to lunge across the table and choke Burton. According to Darby, I didn't say anything, but I grasped my plate like a Frisbee and seemed ready to fling my dinner on him.

I don't know what was going through my head. I do remember Lily saying, "Oh, right! The cobbler must be ready! Thank you for reminding us, Dawn!" Then she, Darby, and Delaney dragged me into the kitchen.

Darby kept an eye on me while Lily and Delaney cut up the cobbler and put the pieces on our good dessert plates.

"I know it's important, but you have to remember how busy he is," Lily was saying as I started to calm down. "He's really focused on his studies, and last fall, during the election, he was applying to lots of law schools. He's putting so many hours into planning for his future, it doesn't leave time for much else."

"Like voting?" I asked. "Like the future of the country?"

"Or learning about cool toys and gifts?" Delaney asked.

"Or taking you out to dinner and stuff?" Darby asked.

Lily paused in the middle of lifting a piece of cobbler and looked at each one of us. "Girls, I don't need someone to pamper me. I admire Burton and what he's doing. He takes life seriously. He can make hard decisions and plan for the future."

"Not if he doesn't vote," I pointed out.

Lily let out a long, loud sigh. "The point is, Burton is a grown-up, unlike . . . other people."

Those wavy lines were back on Lily's forehead, and her mouth was kind of scowling. Plus, she sure was making a mess of the cobbler she was cutting.

All the angry feelings buzzing inside me stopped. "Lily? Are you mad at us?"

"We're sorry!" Delaney said.

Darby started hiccupping some more — she tends to do that when she gets worked up.

Lily set down the knife, and her face got soft again. "No. I'm not mad at you. I just wanted tonight to go really well."

So the three of us promised for a second time to be on our best behavior. And we were — at least for a while.

We helped clear the table and carry out the dessert. I didn't dump any cobbler on Burton, even though I kind of wanted to and had the chance. And no one talked politics.

Instead, as soon as everyone was digging into the cobbler, Mom turned to Lily and asked, "So! How are the wedding plans coming along?"

"Good," Lily said between bites.

"Have you decided on a place?" Dad asked.

"Not yet," Lily replied. "Somewhere small and sweet, I hope."

Mrs. Caldwell seemed to pop up two inches in her chair. "Small? How small?"

"Oh, you know," Lily said. She seemed a little surprised. "Someplace intimate."

"Well, it has to be able to fit everyone."

The M-shaped lines reappeared on Lily's forehead. "I don't think we'll invite more than family and close friends. I'm guessing we'll have only about fifty guests."

"Oh no no no." Mrs. Caldwell shook her head. "You'll have two hundred at least. Possibly more."

Lily looked over at Burton, but he just kept smiling blankly and chewing his cobbler. "I guess . . . I guess we should look into some bigger places."

"And do it soon," Mrs. Caldwell said, waving her fork at Lily as if it were a long metal finger. "Time is running out to plan a summer wedding, and most venues have booked up ages ago."

I was considering my own fork and whether or not it could catapult a piece of warm cobbler between Mrs. Caldwell's eyes. I looked around to see if anyone else was feeling the same way I did, but everyone was staring down at their dessert. (Which was weird because, even though it's delicious, Mom's cobbler isn't all that pretty.)

"Oh, well," Lily said with a laugh. "At least we finished applying for the marriage license."

"A license?" I repeated. I had no idea married people needed a license. "Did you have to take a test?" I'd heard that people who wanted a driver's license had to drive around the block and park between two poles. Maybe people who wanted to get married had to do something that married people do. Like kiss or talk about the bills.

Lily smiled at me. "No, there's no test. You just go down to the county courthouse and fill out a form."

Out of the corner of my eye, I saw Delaney pop up in her chair, much like Mrs. Caldwell did earlier. It was as if our supper table were turning into a game of Whac-A-Mole.

I turned toward her, and so did Darby, but all she did was make big bug eyes at us. I mouthed, *What?* but she didn't say anything. Because right then, we were ushered into the living room to watch Mom open her hostess gift from Mrs. Caldwell.

It was a framed photo of Lily and Burton. Mom passed it around for everyone to see. I couldn't *ooh* or *aah* over it, though. I mean, yes, it was thoughtful. And yes, it was a lovely frame. But when I looked at it, all I could see was Lily with faint squiggles on her forehead sitting next to a giant armadillo.

CHAPTER SEVEN

Court of Appeal

Delaney

When we finally got upstairs, Dawn and Darby asked me to explain the big bug eyes I made at the dinner table. I told them that when Burton and Lily talked about their marriage license, it reminded me that Alex was working as a clerk in the courthouse for the summer — the very same courthouse where they applied for their license!

"Maybe he can do something to stop it," I said as I bounced on my bed. "Like maybe he'll notice they didn't check the right box or something and then their marriage would be illegal?"

"Or he could stamp a big, red *DENIED* on it," Darby said.

"Or he could tear it up into tiny pieces," Dawn said. She let out a loud sigh and shook her head. "I still can't believe they don't have to take a test for something as important as marriage. Sometimes government fails us."

We decided to go visit Alex at his job the very next day.

Mom always lets us walk to Ever's store and the library when we want to — and the courthouse is just three blocks farther — so we figured we didn't need to ask permission. We ate breakfast and waited until Mom started working at her desk. She's a bookkeeper, which sort of sounds like she's a librarian, but it isn't the same thing. They really should call it a budgeter or bill payer. Anyway, some days she has only a little work to do and some days she is at her computer all day, making pages full of numbers, and mumbling. Today looked as if it was going to be a mumbly day, which was good for us.

We waited until she got that look of tremendous focus. You can tell by her eyebrows. They push together right above her nose like a couple of fuzzy, head-butting caterpillars. That's when you know she's lost in the numbers.

"Mom, we're going to town for a little while, okay?" Dawn said.

"Mmm-hmm," she said, still staring at the screen. "Be back by lunchtime." We were stepping through the door when she added, "And don't come back dirty or muddy!"

We walked along Nugent Road toward the middle of town, keeping to the left-hand side the way Lily always taught us. Along the way, we passed the Neighbors, who live opposite Ms. Woolcott. For a long time, we thought Mom, Dad, and Lily just never bothered to learn the names of the nice older couple in the white farmhouse. Then at some point, we realized Neighbor really was their last name.

Mr. Neighbor was in his front yard, chasing squirrels away from his bird feeder.

"Make way for ducklings!" he called out to us as we passed his house. He always says this. He makes fun of the way we walk single file for a couple of blocks until there's more room for us to be side by side and not stick out into the road. We don't mind, though, since he's nice and we always loved the picture book.

"Good morning, Mr. Neighbor," I said.

"Good morning," he said back. "I've got the water going. You're welcome to run around in it."

He nodded toward the sprinklers in his backyard. His sprinklers are much more fun than ours. Last year, Mom exchanged the ones that spray in a circle for underground ones that just pop up and go *whoosh*. But Mr.

Neighbor still has the circle ones. Dawn, Darby, and I like to run around in a game of keep-away from each other and the water. Quincy always hears us and joins in, which makes one more obstacle. We always end up sopping wet and covered in grass. Then Mrs. Neighbor usually comes out and gives us some of her homemade ice cream.

Dawn, Darby, and I all think this is just about the best way to spend a summer day, so when he offered, we stopped to confer. It was getting hot. And Mom didn't say anything about getting wet, so we could get off on a technicality. Eventually, we decided that the courthouse wouldn't look too kindly on triplets that showed up dripping wet and grassy, and our mission was much too important, so we politely declined and continued on our way.

Twenty minutes later, we were at the big brick Blanco County Courthouse. By then, the sun was higher and hotter, and we were so sweaty Dawn said we might as well have gotten wet from the sprinklers. We stood in the shade of the north entryway and fanned each other with a *Thrifty Nickel* someone had left on the steps, until our faces weren't pink anymore and most of the sweat had dried. Then we headed through the doors to the building.

Inside, it was real quiet, and it took us a while to find someone. Eventually we peeked into a room and saw a lady sitting at a desk. In a chair against the wall was a guard reading a newspaper. The lady glanced up at us and got the same wide-eyed, rabbity look that Ms. Caldwell had when she met us. Since Johnson City has less than two thousand residents, most of them either know us or know about us. She must not have been from around here.

"Excuse me. Can I help you?" she said, looking at each of us in turn. People tend to do that. It's like they can't decide which one of us to talk to, so they glance at each of us for a little while and then repeat the process, making them look like oscillating fans.

Dawn stepped forward and cleared her throat the way she does when she feels like she's the boss. "Yes, you may. We are here to see Mr. Alexander Hawthorne."

"And . . . what is this regarding?"

"We can't tell you that," I said.

"What she means is" — Dawn leaned in front of me — "it's a personal matter."

The lady and the security guard exchanged looks. He was grinning and she was pressing her lips together the way people do when they want to keep from laughing. "I see," she said. "Is it a matter of life or death?"

"Life," Darby said. "It's a matter of life. Two lives hang in the balance. And maybe a third, too — a lesser, armadillo-ish one."

Now the lady just looked confused. "One moment." She stood and headed out of the room. A minute later, she returned with Alex.

"These are the young ladies I was telling you about," she said to him. "Apparently, they are having problems with an armadillo."

"Hey there," he said when he saw us. He was smiling big, but his eyes were all bewildered. For some reason, everyone seemed simultaneously happy and puzzled to see us. "What are you three doing here? Is everything okay?"

"No, it's not okay," Dawn said. "Everything is dreadful."

"Horrific," Darby said.

"Appalling," I said. "And only you can stop it."

"Should I call for help?" Alex looked really worried. He glanced over at the security guard, but the man had disappeared behind his newspaper again.

"No, we just need you, Alex," Darby said.

"You're the only one who can help," I said.

"It won't take long," Dawn said. "I promise."

Alex looked over at the lady and she shrugged. "Perhaps you'd better go with them."

He nodded. "I'll be back soon."

As soon as we headed down the front steps of the courthouse, Alex turned to us and said, "So what's going on? You've got me all nervous."

"Is there somewhere we can go to talk?" Dawn said.

Alex glanced at his watch. "I can take an early lunch break. How about we head to Ever's for a bite and you can tell me what this is all about?"

"Great!" we said at the same time, and the four of us started down the sidewalk.

Except I skipped instead of walked because I was so happy. Now that Alex said he would help us, I felt sure everything would be okay. And that hopeful feeling made my feet boing instead of take steps.

Only, I shouldn't have celebrated early. It's like when the House of Representatives wants to pass a bill. Sometimes the right thing to do can be so obvious, but it still isn't easy making it happen.

CHAPTER EIGHT

Counter Strike

Darby

Fifteen minutes later, we were sitting at Forever's front counter. Alex had ordered the lunch special — half a pimento cheese sandwich and a helping of homemade coleslaw — and the three of us ordered slices of pie. Dawn ordered a slice of apple pie (of course), and Delaney ordered a slice of the chocolate icebox pie (also of course). Forever's has their pies on display, and I always order the one that is least popular because I feel sorry for it. It's weird, I know, but that's what I do. Today, it was rhubarb pie. It was really good, but for some reason, I couldn't eat much. The whole time we explained our plan to Alex, my stomach kept getting squeezier and squeezier until I set down my fork and gave up altogether.

It was the same with Alex. As we told him our idea about the marriage license, he ate more and more slowly until he finally stopped. When we were done, he sat silent for a while. Then he said, "Girls, I can't do that."

"Why not?"

He let out a long sigh. "For so many reasons. First of all, it's unethical and highly illegal. Surely you understand that it's against the law to willfully destroy government property, right?"

"We just wanted you to reject their application," Dawn said.

"Or spill coffee on it," I said.

"Or accidentally knock it into the shredder," Delaney said.

"Also, I don't work in that department," Alex went on. "It would look hugely suspicious for me to go snooping."

"Well . . . we could provide a distraction," Dawn suggested. "Delaney could get stuck in a tree again."

Delaney sat up straight. "Yes! I could. I'm good at screaming loud, too."

"But most of all, even if I could do it, I wouldn't." Alex looked each one of us in the eyes. "This is what your sister wants. You have to accept it."

"But it's Burton!" Dawn said. "The poopiest of nincompoops!"

Alex sighed. "Look. I get it. He's a couple of years older, so I never got to know him that well, but I agree that he doesn't seem to have a lot in common with Lily. . . ." His voice trailed off and for a moment he just sat there, frowning at the remains of his coleslaw. Then he shook his head and continued. "The thing is, all that doesn't matter. If you love your sister, you'll support her decision. Lily is a wonderful person. She's smart and kind and perceptive and beautiful. . . . She wouldn't marry someone for no good reason. So he can't be all bad. Right?"

"He's not," I said. Dawn and Delaney immediately gave me the stink eye. "Well, it's true. He's not an evil villain. He's just . . . not you, Alex. He doesn't make Lily laugh."

"He doesn't like dogs or flowers. And he gives lousy gifts," Delaney grumbled.

"His mom wants Lily to wear a toilet-seat ring!" Dawn whined. "And his favorite president is" — she glanced left and right, leaned forward, and whispered — "Franklin Pierce."

"But he loves Lily," Alex said. "He sees how special she is. That means he's pretty smart and has good taste, right?"

Dawn and I shrugged. "I guess," Delaney mumbled.

"And he makes her happy. No matter how you feel about him, that's the most important thing. Doesn't she deserve happiness?"

Dawn frowned down at her pie. Delaney looked over at me.

"Yes," I said. "She does. Lots of it."

Alex smiled a sad type of smile. "So you understand why I can't do this for you, right?"

"Yes," we all mumbled.

"Good." He rose to his feet and checked the time on his cell phone. "I'm afraid it's time for me to head back. It was good to see all of you."

The three of us exchanged fearful looks. Our plan had failed. We weren't prepared for this.

"You aren't mad at us, are you?" I asked.

Alex shook his head. "No way. You guys love your sister and want to protect her. That's a good thing." He pushed in his chair. "Okay, one last bit of trivia before I go. Ready? Tallest president?"

"Lincoln!" we all said together.

"Shortest president?"

"Madison!"

He laughed. "You guys give me faith in the future — you know that? Just . . . no more plotting criminal activities, okay?"

Then he turned and walked back to the courthouse. I felt so sad watching him go. It was the same wobbly sensation I got when Lily left for college, and when Daddy moved out of the house for good. As if someone grabbed the world and shook it like a snow globe, stirring everything up.

"Well, I'm convinced," Dawn said.

"About what?" I asked.

"It's so clear," Dawn said.

"What are you talking about? Nothing's clear. Everything is wrong and it's about to get wronger!" The skin around Delaney's eyes was all cotton-candy pink — the way it gets when she, or any of us, is about to cry. Apparently, I wasn't the only one who felt gloomy.

"It's obvious that Alex is still in love with Lily," Dawn said. "Don't you see how soft his eyes get when he talks about her? Didn't you notice the tone in his voice? It was so . . ."

"Mournful," Delaney said.

"Anguished," I said.

Dawn tapped her finger on her chin. "Heartbroken, I'd say."

The more I thought about it, the more I realized those signs were unmistakable. Delaney was nodding, too. And the rosy color around her eyes had disappeared.

"Now we really have to stop the wedding," Dawn said. "Not just for Lily but for Alex, too. Agreed?"

Delaney and I nodded. "Agreed."

CHAPTER NINE

Summit

Delaney

The entire walk home, we tried to think of new ways to stop the wedding. Dawn was the only one who came up with a plan, but we decided that hiring someone to kidnap Burton was probably too expensive. Plus, it was most likely illegal, and we'd just promised Alex we'd stop that stuff.

We were starting to feel panicky. It was like that feeling we get right before school starts. We always start the summer with plans to build a fort, teach Quincy circus tricks, and make a movie about *Marbury v. Madison*. But then August comes around and we realize all we've really done is watch lots of cartoons.

The closer we got to our house, the worse we felt. The Neighbors were sitting on their front porch as we passed and again invited us to play keep-away in their sprinklers, and again we politely declined. A few steps later, Darby pointed toward our backyard and said, "Look!"

There, sitting on the hill behind our house, was Lily. She was in her favorite spot — underneath the red oak, staring out at the hills. She particularly loves it during the sunset, but that wasn't supposed to happen for another eight hours or so. Which could only mean . . .

Sure enough, Lily was crying. She sat cross-legged in the shade of the red oak, and a pile of wadded-up Kleenex sat in the middle of her lap. Quincy was also there, in the shade of another tree. He lay with his head on his front legs, watching Lily closely, as if he were worried about her, too.

Darby plopped down beside Lily and wrapped an arm around her. "What's wrong?"

"Oh, don't mind me," Lily said, wiping her cheeks. "I'm just being silly."

"No, you aren't. Why are you sad?"

Lily reached for another Kleenex and started dabbing at her eyes. "It's nothing. I just . . . I was thinking about how much I'm going to miss this place."

"But where are you going?" I asked.

"I'm getting married, silly. When you marry someone, you go live with them. By Labor Day, I'll be in Chicago."

Dawn, Darby, and I traded looks of alarm. We'd forgotten that part. We'd been focusing so much on the wedding and how much we didn't want it to happen, we forgot that it led to a marriage — marriage to a blockhead in a faraway place. And we had no plan to stop it, which meant it was really going to happen. We'd lose Lily *and* Alex!

Who was going to play Presidential Trivia with us now? Who was going to hug us and teach us how to watch out for small-town traffic? Who was going to buy us pie and tell us to not commit felonies?

Darby held Lily tighter and started crying. Then I started blubbering and plopped down on the other side of Lily and held on to her. Dawn, being Dawn, tried to fight it. She stood there with her mouth bunched up and her hands balled up into fists, but tears were already running down her cheeks.

"Don't go, Lily!" Darby said. "Don't get married and move away!"

"But I have to," Lily said.

"You don't! Look how sad it's making you," I pointed out.

Lily moved her mouth a few different ways and then finally said, "It's complicated."

"Don't say that!" Dawn said. "You never used to say things like that. Just tell us — please?"

"You're right. I'm sorry. I just mean that it's hard to describe. You can be happy and excited about a new change but also sad to say good-bye to people and places you love."

Dawn couldn't take it anymore. She burst out crying. And because Lily didn't have any sides left, Dawn plunked down behind her and hugged her from the back. That got me and Darby wailing again, and I could tell by her shuddering movements that Lily had restarted, too.

So there we all sat, sobbing and hanging on to Lily like baby possums. I heard a whiny noise and Quincy was there. He flung his big square head into Lily's lap and whimpered along with the rest of us. Lily couldn't have moved if she'd wanted to. And I started to have silly thoughts about us getting stuck like that and how then she couldn't marry Burton and move away — because we had become a giant sister-dog-ball.

After a while, we stopped crying and slowly pulled apart. Only Quincy stayed put. In fact, he crawled completely across Lily's lap and took the opportunity to nap. The rest of us sat there, sniffling.

"I'm sorry, girls," Lily said. "I didn't mean to upset you. Everything's all right. I'm just feeling a little overwhelmed."

"How so?" I asked.

"There's so much to do for the wedding. I have to book the place and do a rush order on the invitations and pick out bridesmaids dresses and see if I can find a violinist. I'm scared I won't have enough time to do it all."

Dawn made a harrumphing noise. "Why doesn't Burton help you?"

"He's finishing up this paper for his degree and also trying to get it published — it's really important to him, and he has to spend as much time as possible in the library. I just can't bother him with things like this."

"I'll help you!" Dawn said.

Darby and I snuck her looks that said *Why?* and *Are you crazy?* But she ignored us.

"Would you? That would be so sweet!"

Lily looked so much less stressed than she did just a few minutes before, I found myself saying, "Sure. We'll all help."

"Just tell us everything you need to do to plan the wedding and we'll see what we can help with," Dawn said. Her eyes met mine for the tiniest of seconds. But in that instant, I understood. This wasn't just about making Lily feel better. This was about gathering intelligence so we could stop the wedding.

I know that makes us sound selfish and wicked and all-around bad, but that's how much we love Lily and didn't want to lose her. Lily, who taught us how to walk like ducklings down the road so we wouldn't get hit by cars. Lily, who let us all cram into her tiny bed when we used to be scared of thunderstorms. Lily, who was right then scratching Quincy's belly and comforting him, even though he kept passing gas.

Lily. The best big sister in the world.

CHAPTER TEN

Covert Actions

Dawn

So we finally had another plan. "Operation Postpone," we called it.

The day after our big cry fest, Lily shared with us her list of wedding tasks, and it turned out that she still hadn't found a place to hold the wedding. We watched as she called a few places and left messages on voice mail. Then she had to drive to Austin to see about hiring a musician to play "Here Comes the Bride." Since she would be on the road, and Mom was working, Lily asked us to answer the phone if anyone called back about a venue. We told her we would, but secretly we'd already sworn a triplet oath to prevent any booking from happening.

The way we figured it, if Lily couldn't find any place to hold the wedding, she'd have no choice but to delay it — which was almost as good as canceling it. That would buy us more time to talk her out of marrying Burton.

I guess I should have felt bad about our deception, especially since Lily seemed so relieved to have help, but I didn't. At least what we were doing wasn't against the law.

"You should be able to reach me on my cell phone in a couple of hours," she said as we stood on the front porch. "If anyone calls, take messages for me. Mom has credit card information if they need that, but try not to disturb her otherwise. Oh, and Mrs. Caldwell is coming over this evening to help, so please play hostess if I'm not back yet."

"Oh joy," I mumbled, but only Delaney heard me.

Lily then hugged us and drove away. Before her white Toyota had disappeared from view, we could hear the phone ringing inside. There was a little jam in the doorway as all three of us ran for it at once. Delaney got there first.

"Hello? Yes, this is the Brewster residence," we heard her say. "Yes. . . . Really? . . . So you're all booked up?" Delaney gave us a big smile and a thumbs-up. "No, that's totally okay. Thank you so much! Good-bye."

She hung up the phone and then bounced up and down on her toes, saying, "No go! No go! North Oak

Inn is a no-go!" Soon we were all bouncing up and down, chanting along with her, until Mom came in and asked us what we were carrying on about. Delaney said "nothing," that we were just playing a silly game. Mom reminded us of the time we got so caught up in a reenactment of the Kennedy assassination that Ms. Woolcott got worried and called the sheriff.

"Besides, I have deadlines and can't risk getting a headache, your sister is stressed over this wedding, and Mrs. Caldwell is coming over and she already thinks we're a house full of barbarians," she added.

As soon as we looked adequately sorry and agreed to keep our voices down to non-worrisome and non-irritating levels, Mom thanked us and left.

Then the phone rang again. This time, Darby grabbed it. It was the Elks Lodge, which was sad to inform us that their clubhouse was not available until October. This time, we celebrated with a silent dance and soft high fives. The next couple of hours were full of rejoicing. When Hochmeister's Biergarten called to say they weren't available, we had ice cream and clinked our spoons together. When the SPJST Hall said they had only two dates in September open, we ran to the front yard to do cartwheels.

We also took turns checking off venues from the list Lily left. By three o'clock, there was only one place left on the page. We were sitting in the living room, playing Spite and Malice, when the phone rang again. I grabbed it before the others could. Sure enough, it was some lady asking for Lily.

"She isn't in right now, but this is her sister Dawn. May I take a message?"

"This is Shirley down at the Bluebonnet House. Please tell her we got her message and are happy to host her wedding."

"Really?" I suddenly felt really heavy and sank down into the nearby armchair. "Are you sure?" I gave my sisters a distress-signal look. Darby's eyes got big, and Delaney mouthed the words *Oh no!*

The lady chuckled. "Why, yes! We had an event cancellation only yesterday. I'll just need the deposit and a bit more information. Do you know how many guests there will be?"

A teeny lightbulb — like the size you find on a strand of Christmas lights — blinked on in my mind. "Um . . . I think about five hundred," I said.

"Five hundred?" she repeated. "Five hundred people? Are you sure?"

"Oh yes," I replied, feeling a little more confident. "At least that many. We have a very big family and lots of friends."

"Dear me. I don't think we can fit a crowd that size. . . . And the parking . . ."

"Don't worry about the parking," I said. "Most of us will ride up on horseback."

"Horseback?"

"Yes, Lily insists. She's a big animal lover. In fact, our dog, Quincy, is going to be the best man." Quincy, who had been snoozing under the nearby table, lifted his head and looked at me. I tried not to laugh. Delaney, in the meantime, had both of her hands clamped over her mouth and was bright red from holding in her giggles.

"I'm afraid there are health codes we have to follow," the lady said. "I just don't think we can host such an event. I'm so sorry. Is there any way your sister might change her mind on some of these things? Might I speak with her later, when she returns?"

"I highly doubt she will change her mind. And I'm not sure when she'll be back. She's in Austin looking to hire . . . bagpipe players. For the music."

At this, Delaney let out a snorting sound so loud, Quincy jumped to his feet and glanced around for the wild animal. It took every bit of power in every one of my cells to not crack up.

"Well, then, I'm afraid we simply cannot help her," the lady said. "I am very sorry. Please pass along my regrets. We wish her luck with her . . . um . . . her everything."

As soon as I hung up the phone, I collapsed onto the rug, laughing. Darby and Delaney flopped down next to me and we rolled around guffawing and hooting and forgetting to be quiet until Mom came out and gave us a scary warning look.

"Is that it?" I asked after Mom went back to her office. "Is that all of the venues?"

Darby rolled over to the coffee table and snatched Lily's list. "Yep. That's all of them."

The three of us looked at each other. Then Delaney said, "We did it. We really did it. Now they have to delay the wedding."

"And that will give us time to convince Lily she's making a mistake," I said.

"And get her and Alex together," Darby added.

This got us all excited again, so we went outside, where we could whoop and holler and turn cartwheels and not disturb Mom. Eventually, the heat forced us back inside for some iced tea. We were in the middle of debating whether to celebrate with a trip to Forever's for more pie or a romp in the sprinklers, when Lily walked in.

"So how did it go?" she asked, hanging her purse on the hook by the back door. "Did anyone call?"

She looked so tired, and all at once I didn't feel like celebrating anymore. I remembered how stressed and sad she was the day before, and how we'd promised to help her. Suddenly, I felt ashamed. I could tell by the way Darby and Delaney slumped in their seats that they felt the same way.

Lily noticed, too. Those wavy lines reappeared on her forehead. "Dawn?" she said, looking right at me.

Just because I like to take charge, I'm also the one people turn to when the others go silent. That's the part I don't like about being the eldest triplet.

I picked up the list of venues — the one we'd just taken turns hugging and dancing around with — and handed it to her. "I'm sorry, Lily," I said. "They called back, but none of them can do the wedding."

She took the paper from my hands and stared at it. "Oh," she said. All that tightness and tension that had been in her face the day before came back. Her shoulders hunched and she plunked down on a nearby stool with a sigh. It was like watching a flower wilt. I felt like a scoundrel.

"I'm sorry, Lily!" Darby said.

Lily seemed startled. "Girls, no. Please don't apologize. You did me a big favor today. It's not your fault that the news is all bad." Then she gave us all hugs and went into her room.

The three of us trudged up the stairs to the Triangular Office.

"Man, I feel lousy," I said. "Like a real rat."

"A weasel," Darby said.

"A lowly slug," Delaney said.

The three of us flopped on our beds and didn't say another word. We could hear Lily and Mom talking downstairs. A little while later, the doorbell rang and we could hear the shrill, chickenlike sounds of Mrs. Caldwell talking.

It was the most upside-down and inside-out day ever. None of us knew how to feel. We didn't want Lily to marry Burton, but we didn't want her to be unhappy and stressed either. I considered telling her about the Bluebonnet House and how she could probably book the wedding there if she explained that she wouldn't be inviting half the town or including any four-legged guests — only I didn't know if that would make me feel better or worse, or if that was truly the best thing for Lily or not.

Before I could decide, Mom called us down to dinner.

Mrs. Caldwell was still squawking. "Austin is only fifty miles away, after all. And Fredericksburg and Marble Falls are even closer," she was saying. "People don't mind a short drive, especially for something this important."

"But it's high season right now," Mom said. "Most places have probably been booked way in advance."

Lily was staring out the dining room window toward the hill behind our house. Her face looked all pulled-down and sad. All that shame and regret was building to a bursting point inside me, and I was just about to open my mouth and confess when Lily whirled around.

"I know what to do," she said. Her eyes were all shiny and determined.

Mom and Mrs. Caldwell stopped jabbering. "What?" Mom asked.

"We should have it here." Lily spread out her arms.

Mrs. Caldwell shook her head. "Goodness, no. This place simply isn't large enough. You can't fit two hundred people here."

"We can do it if we cut down on guests," Lily said. "It's that or push back the wedding until Christmas break — or next summer."

"Well, we certainly can't have that," Mrs. Caldwell said. "Burton is moving this fall."

Lily looked at Mom, who now had wavy forehead lines of her own. "Please? Can't we have it here? We'll keep it small and simple, I promise." She nodded at the three of us. "And you guys will help. Right?"

Darby, Delaney, and I looked at each other. In our telepathic triplet way, I knew they felt the same way I did: totally thwarted but relieved to see light in Lily's eyes again. And unable to say no to her.

"Sure," we said at the same time.

"Well, then. I guess that settles it," Mom said. "The wedding is back on."

CHAPTER ELEVEN

Confirmation Hearing

Darby

The next day was the start of a Dad weekend, and since he always keeps us busy with stuff, we didn't have much time to plot and plan. It was constantly on my mind, though. As we watched a movie about an invasion of buglike aliens, I kept thinking that the upside to extra-terrestrials taking over Earth would be that Lily would probably have to call off the wedding. As we took turns getting rides with Dad on the Vespa, I kept picturing Lily hopping on the scooter and being driven far away — so far that by the time she made her way back to Johnson City, it would be too late for the wedding. And when he took us out for ice cream, and I saw a girl and guy about Lily's age holding hands, I imagined Lily running into Alex at the ice-cream shop and falling in love with him all over again.

"Okay. What's up with you three?" Daddy said as we sat in the booth at the ice-cream parlor. "I've never seen you girls so quiet."

The three of us looked at each other. No one wanted to answer.

"Dawn?" Daddy said, looking right at her.

She checked my eyes and Delaney's to make sure it was all right to talk and said, "We don't want Lily to get married."

"I see." Dad sat back against the red vinyl booth. "Why not?"

"Because she's going to move away!" Dawn said, pushing aside her ice cream as if in protest.

Dad nodded. "I don't like that either," he said. "But it happens a lot when you marry someone. It's how I ended up in Johnson City."

That was true. Our house has been in our mom's family for generations — she grew up there and so did her mom and so did *her* mother. Daddy was what Mom called a "city boy" she met when she went to UT. When he asked her to marry him, she made it clear that she wanted to raise her kids on the family homestead. He agreed and moved out here with her.

"Also, we don't like how stressed out Lily is over the wedding," I said.

Again, Daddy nodded. "It's a lot of work and she doesn't have a lot of time. Most brides get to feeling overwhelmed by it all. Lily told me you three have been helping her out. That makes me proud."

"Except we hate Burton!" Delaney said.

Daddy looked surprised. But, then, so did Dawn and I. We weren't prepared for her to blurt out the truth.

"You hate him?" Daddy's eyebrows lifted so high, they disappeared under the baseball cap he likes to wear to hide his bald spot.

Dawn and I shifted guiltily in the booth, and the red vinyl made loud, embarrassing noises.

"Yes," Delaney said. "He's boring and nervous and hates the outdoors and never holds Lily's hand or takes her to get pie. I don't like his mom. I don't like his presents. And I hate his squinty armadillo face!"

"Wow," Daddy mumbled.

Dawn and I slumped down in our seats. But that was hard to do secretly because of the big flatulent sounds it made. That Delaney and her big mouth! Now Daddy would lecture us for the whole weekend and tell Mom when he dropped us off so that she could pick up where he left off.

"Is that how you feel, too?" Daddy asked me and Dawn.

We nodded. There was no use denying it. We told him that we didn't exactly hate him, we just hated that he was taking Lily away from us, and we thought he was all wrong for her.

"You know how when the president wants to give someone an important job in the administration, they hold a big meeting and ask that person lots of questions? And then, if they don't like the answers they hear, they can vote no and the president has to find someone else for the job?" I asked.

"You mean the Senate confirmation hearings?" Daddy asked.

"Yeah. Those. Well, how come we can't have that for the job of Lily's husband? How come we can't sit him down and ask him lots of questions?"

I thought maybe Daddy would laugh at me, but he didn't. He sat forward and looked interested. "What would you ask him?" he said.

Dawn, Delaney, and I started suggesting all kinds of questions, like . . . What would he do if Lily were sad? What if Lily wanted to plant flowers around their house? What if she wanted to visit her family? What if she wanted a pet rabbit — or ten? Would he make sure she smiled and laughed every day? Would he give her thoughtful birthday presents? Would he keep her out of harm's way?

The whole time, Daddy listened quietly. Then, when we ran out of questions to suggest, he said, "All right. Let's say you sat him down at the booth here, and you asked him all of those things. Let's say he promised to do everything he could to keep Lily happy and safe. Let's say he agreed to take care of her, with a nice house, and any flowers or pets she wants, and as many visits to her family as she wants. And say he gave his word that he would consult with all of us before buying Lily a gift. Would you like him then?"

Again we went all fidgety. And again the vinyl seat made loud *brrrap!* noises.

"I don't know," Dawn said eventually. "I think he'd still be all wrong."

Delaney and I nodded. That's how we felt, too.

"Okay, then, let's say we put Lily on the stand," Daddy said. "I mean, it would only be fair, right? What should we ask her?"

For a long time, none of us answered him. We just shrugged and *brrrapped* and twirled our ice-cream spoons. It was fair, but we didn't like the idea of Lily being interrogated.

"We should ask her —" I stopped, unsure if I really wanted to say it aloud. Then I decided to just go ahead and do it. "We should ask her if she's still in love with Alex."

Everyone fell silent again. Even the vinyl didn't make any noise. It was the most glum I'd ever felt while eating a hot fudge sundae.

After a while, Daddy took off his cap, and rubbed his forehead, and put his cap back on. Then he let out a long sigh and said, "You know what? You girls are right. Marriage shouldn't be entered into without lots and lots of thought."

His eyes looked sad as he said this, and I had a big urge to hug him. It made me wonder if he was talking about his and Mom's marriage or Lily's — or both.

"Plus, I think you're right about something else," he said.

"What?" we all asked.

"Burton does sort of look like an armadillo."

We laughed. Then the three of us took turns giving him hugs.

CHAPTER TWELVE

Ways and Means

Dawn

On Monday, we were back at Mom's doing chores. Lots of chores. More chores than we'd ever done before. And since Lily was busy getting the big white dress altered to fit, it all came down to us triplets.

I think Mom was a little freaked at the thought of hosting a wedding there. I totally understand that, but I didn't see why we had to clean places that the wedding guests would never see. Like the pantry. And the hall closet. And the laundry room. I ask you, what kind of tomfool would wash his clothes at a wedding?

Poor Quincy kept running from room to room, trying to find a quiet spot where he could nap. Eventually, he whined to go outside and crawled into his kennel on the porch.

At one point, Mom asked us to load the dishes in the dishwasher while she got out a ladder and cleaned the light fixtures in the living room. We were doing fine until we realized we were out of dishwasher detergent. Darby suggested using the liquid soap Mom used to wash dishes by hand, so we squirted a bunch in the tray and started the machine.

We then went outside to take a break and check on poor Quincy. When Delaney went back in to get him a treat, we heard her scream. Darby and I ran inside and found that the kitchen was full of bubbles, piles of them, almost as tall as we were.

"Turn off the dishwasher!" Delaney shouted. Only, we couldn't even see the dishwasher. So we had to dive into the bubbles and feel around for the OFF switch. It was tough because the floor was all slippery, but eventually someone hit the right button and it stopped. That's when we heard Mom's surprised yelp.

Boy, was she mad. She made us go up to the Triangular Office to change clothes and clean our room — although we couldn't imagine how any of the wedding guests would end up in there.

"I feel like Cinderella," I said, scanning the mess around us.

"I feel like Rapunzel," Darby said, staring out the

window over the porch. Sunshine lit up the foamy bubbles that still clung to her braids.

"I feel like Jack who fell down and broke his crown," Delaney grumbled, rubbing a spot on her forehead from when she slipped in the bubbles and banged it against a cabinet. "I don't know why Mom's sore at us. She wanted to mop the floor anyway."

We talked about how Lily's stress had spread to Mom and us and Quincy, and we wondered aloud if it might continue to build upward and outward — just like the bubbles — until it took over the whole town, and Johnson City became a village of cantankerous dunderheads. But even though we were sort of being punished, we were glad to be in our room, the same way Quincy had decided he preferred his kennel on the porch.

After we pushed all the clutter under our beds and into our closet and played a couple of games of Spite and Malice, Lily came upstairs. She was laughing.

"Mom told me about the dishwasher," she said between giggles.

It was so good to see. She hadn't cracked up like that in a really long time.

"Is Mom laughing?" I asked.

"Um . . . not yet."

She told us that Burton and his mom were coming over to help work on the guest list and that we were allowed to go downstairs again.

I answered the door when Burton and Mrs. Caldwell rang the bell. As usual, he was holding his satchel of papers. She was smiling and holding a white box. "I have a surprise," she said, walking right past me over to Lily and Mom.

Darby, Delaney, and I all gathered around. I knew they were thinking the same thing — that Mrs. Caldwell had stopped at Forever's for a pie or some pecan tarts.

She lifted the lid, but all we could see were rows of cards. "Ta-da!" Mrs. Caldwell said, holding one up. "Your invitations are done!"

"But . . . I thought I would pick them out," Lily said.

"Mother knew you were busy, so she figured she'd take care of it herself," Burton said. "Isn't that thoughtful?"

"You and Burton can go ahead and address them while you work on the guest list tonight, and they'll be ready to mail tomorrow," Mrs. Caldwell said. "Aren't they lovely?" She pulled one out of the box to show us. "There are even a few with special inserts that tell all about the rehearsal dinner."

"But . . . why are they that color?" Delaney asked. "I didn't think wedding invitations came in gray."

Mrs. Caldwell looked miffed. "They aren't gray. The color is 'stardust.' They are more a silvery hue."

I squinted at it. "Reminds me of a gravestone," I said.

"They're . . . they're . . ." Darby's voice was all quivery, the way it gets when she's trying not to laugh. "They're armadillo-colored!"

Sure enough, she started cracking up. But then, so did Delaney and I.

"Girls! That's enough," Mom said. "I think perhaps you better go to your room."

"But we just got down here," I said.

"And back up you'll go, until you learn how to behave."

"But . . . but . . ." I looked at Lily. Her face was bright pink and she was staring at the floor. To her left stood Burton, blowing his nose as usual. And to his left stood Mrs. Caldwell, who was trying hard to not look at me or Darby or Delaney. Instead, she focused on the wall above us. Her mouth was all bunched up like the top of a drawstring bag.

"Go. Up. Now," Mom said. She wasn't yelling, but it was almost worse than yelling. It was the quiet voice of someone with a whole lot of yelling trapped inside them.

Without another word, we went upstairs.

"That's not fair!" I said, slamming the door to the Triangular Office. "We didn't do anything wrong. It's not our fault Mrs. Caldwell ordered ugly invitations."

"Yeah," Darby said. "And besides, that was supposed to be Lily's job. No one asked Mrs. Caldwell to butt in."

Delaney paced back and forth in front of the window. "Lily would never have chosen gray. She would have picked out buttercup yellow or honeysuckle pink — something nice. And did you see the writing? It was so shiny and curly, I couldn't even read it."

"Yeah," Darby and I said at the same time.

Little by little, my anger seemed to dwindle away, like the hot water in Mom's bathroom shower, until I just felt tired and defeated. So I flopped onto my bed.

Soon, Delaney stopped pacing and Darby stopped scowling at the floor and they toppled onto their beds, too. For a moment, we just lay there and made grumbling sounds. Then Delaney said, "I'm awful tired of being stuck in here."

Darby pointed out that we probably wouldn't have any fun downstairs either, since Burton and his mom were visiting and everyone seemed mad at us. Besides, they were just making a guest list and addressing those ugly, cement-colored invitations. It wasn't like we were missing any fun.

I started thinking about the guest list and something kept bugging me. "Lily better invite Alex," I said.

"We've known Alex so long, it's like he's part of the family. He deserves to come," Darby said.

"But he said he'd only come over if Lily invited him," Delaney said. "That probably means the wedding, too."

I sat up. "Then we just have to make sure he gets an invitation."

Darby sat up. "Yeah. Then maybe when he gets it, he'll realize she still cares."

Delaney stood and started bouncing on her toes. "And then Alex will beg her not to marry Burton!"

"We have to do this. It's altogether fitting and proper that we should do it," I said, borrowing a little from Abraham Lincoln. "For Lily. For the family. For . . . the sake of love itself. We shall not let it perish from the earth!"

Darby leaped to her feet and started clapping. Delaney cheered. It was the best and most important speech I'd ever given.

Well, so far anyway.

CHAPTER THIRTEEN

Operation Eaves Drop

Delaney

First off, I want to say that what happened was not my fault. Dawn says it was, and Darby can't remember. But it's not. I will tell you all the facts, just the facts, and nothing but the facts, and you'll see for yourself.

The plan was to make sure Alex received one of those invitations. But we couldn't just steal one and send it. We had to be certain Lily wasn't already planning to ask him. Because if he got two invitations, he'd know for sure that something weird was up. So we decided to eavesdrop.

Now, my sisters and I have gotten really good at eavesdropping over the years. We have all kinds of methods. We know everything about this old house, including places to hide, vents that carry the sounds of voices up to the attic, and cracks that let you hear or watch things. And we're trying to go high-tech, too. Last fall, we pooled our allowance and bought things like walkie-talkies and binoculars. We also got a little recording device we saw advertised in the back of a comic book. We tied it to Quincy's collar and let him wander around. We were hoping to overhear Mom discussing our Christmas gifts, but instead, we got a half hour of Quincy snoring. We're still working out the kinks in that system.

I'm slightly taller and a whole lot faster than the others, so they usually designate me for peeking in windows or for things that require a quick getaway. But it's hard for me to keep still, especially for a long time. So for this mission, someone else was chosen.

"Leave it to me," Dawn said, choosing herself. Something she likes to do — a lot.

From the shadowy spot on the stairwell, Dawn managed to hide long enough to overhear a few things. She found out that Mom and Mrs. Caldwell were going to start addressing cards to family, friends, and other obvious people at the dining room table while Lily and Burton sat on the porch swing and finalized the overall guest list. She also saw Mrs. Caldwell push Quincy away with her foot when she thought no one was looking.

"I almost tackled her," Dawn grumbled when she came back with her report. "But for the good of the mission, I stopped myself."

We decided to eavesdrop on Lily and Burton to see if Alex's name came up. I opened our attic window, which was right over the porch, but all we could hear was some garbled murmuring. Because there was a little roof over the porch, it got in the way of us hearing them.

Now here's the strange thing about Darby. She is the shyest of all of us. She hates talking to people outside of family and once paid Dawn ten dollars to pretend to be her when she had to give an oral report about Presidents' Day to her class. When we were really little, she used to turn completely around in group pictures, because she's camera shy, too. That's why we have so many photos of her backside in between me and Dawn grinning. She faces the front now, but she usually looks down at her shoes.

Anyway, even though she's shy around people, she's also the most courageous one of us in every other way. She isn't afraid of Mom's bathroom ghost, she doesn't run from bugs or rodents or snakes, and if someone dares her to do something, she'll almost always do it. So we weren't surprised when she turned around from the window and said, "I should climb out there."

"I don't know . . ." I said.

"It'll be fine," Darby said. "Y'all can keep hold of my feet while I get out on the roof. I'll be able to hear them from there."

It took a few minutes for her to convince us. Finally, we agreed, mainly because we were running out of time, and it was our only option. But we insisted that she wear a bicycle helmet.

Darby changed into long pants and a long-sleeved shirt, because the porch roof was hot and rough. Then she put her knee pads on over her pants and strapped on her helmet. "Let me climb partway out, and then you grab hold of my legs. Once you have a good grip on me, I'll stretch out farther."

As soon as she climbed out the window, Dawn grabbed hold of her left leg, and I grabbed hold of her right. Darby waited a few seconds and then inched forward, little by little, until she was flat on her stomach.

She glanced back at us. Her face was bright pink, but she had a big gleamy smile on her face. "This is great!" she whisper-shouted.

I just nodded back at her. At that point, Dawn and I only had ahold of her ankles, and I was concentrating too hard on what I was doing to talk back to her. Dawn also didn't say anything.

After a while, I started to get tired. Dawn must have, too, because she whispered, "How much longer?"

"I don't know," I whispered back.

My hands were getting sweaty and I was afraid I might lose my grip.

"Hurry up!" I hissed out the window, but my words seemed to get lost in the breeze. I wasn't sure if Darby heard them.

We continued like that for a while longer, with me trying not to think about itchy spots on my body or all the jitters trapped inside me. Of course, when you try hard to not think about things, you only think about them more.

Then we heard a noise behind us. The tapping of toenails on our wooden floor, followed by low doggie whines.

"Quincy is up here," I whispered.

"I know," said Dawn. "Just ignore him. Poor thing's probably tired of being mistreated by that woman."

I could ignore Quincy, but I was worried that he wouldn't ignore us. Sure enough, a moment later, I could feel a cold wet nose on my calf.

"*Eeep!*" I started. "Go away, Quincy!" But he wouldn't. He just whimpered a little and looked at me with those sad brown eyes. "Git!"

"Ignore him," Dawn commanded without looking at me or him. I could see little glistens of sweat on her forehead and upper lip. She was having a hard time holding on to Darby, too.

I tried to ignore him. I really did. And this next part is not my fault.

What happened was, I closed my eyes and tried to block out everything but my grip on Darby. I tried to forget the itches and that heebie-jeebie, ants-in-the-pants feeling I had. And then Quincy licked me right on the ticklish part of my leg, behind my knee.

I opened my eyes, shouted something like "*Yah!*" and let go of Darby's foot. I didn't mean to — it just happened. I saw her foot disappear out the window, and Darby slid sideways, toward the left. Dawn shouted, "Hey!" and her body started to get pulled through the window.

It all happened so fast, I didn't know how to react. I just sort of screamed, and my arms kept flailing around. I couldn't grab Darby's foot again because it was now too far away. Meanwhile, Quincy kept jumping and turning in circles, thinking I was playing with him.

"Help!" Dawn said as her feet started coming off the floor.

I went to grab her but tripped over Quincy and ended up falling into her instead. That's when she let go of Darby.

We heard a long scraping sound followed by a *whoosh* and someone screaming.

"Oh no!" Dawn cried.

Both of us ran downstairs as fast as we could, Quincy following right behind because he still thought it was part of a game. The whole time, Dawn and I were making little wailing sounds and pushing each other out of the way. I thought for sure we'd just killed our sister.

The first thing I saw when I made it to the porch was Mrs. Caldwell. She was trotting around in little circles, saying "Oh my!" and making the same flapping motions with her arms that I'd been making upstairs. Lily and Mom were at the porch railing, looking down. I raced to their side and saw Darby lying on top of our big althea bush, which was now crushed all to pieces. Leaves and flowers were scattered everywhere, which was probably why Burton was sneezing in the far corner of the porch.

"Don't move!" Mom was saying to Darby.

"But it prickles!" Darby said.

I'd never been so happy to hear her talk in all my life.

Eventually, they decided she didn't have any broken bones and they could help her up. As I started to tromp down the porch steps to help, Mom whirled on me and said, "Stay back! You three have done enough!" Her eyes were like the rockets' red glare.

I sat on the porch swing and watched as Lily and Mom gently pulled Darby to her feet. Mrs. Caldwell stood by the railing and pretended to help by saying things like "Easy now. Watch her head." Burton just kept sneezing.

While I sat there, I saw a paper on the seat next to me. The guest list! Glancing around to make sure no one was looking, I picked it up and checked the names. Alex wasn't on there.

Dawn was peering around the frame of the front door. "Is Darby still alive?" she asked.

I nodded.

Dawn's head disappeared as soon as Mom, Lily, and Darby started coming up the steps. I set down the list and stood up. Darby was covered in leaves, flower petals, and tiny twigs, and she was hiccupping loudly. She also had a funny smile on her face. For a while, they made her move her arms and legs this way and that and peered into her eyes to make sure she was truly all right. Since Burton couldn't stop sneezing, Mrs. Caldwell took him home.

As soon as their car pulled away, Mom said, "What on earth did you girls think you were doing?"

I didn't know what to say, and Dawn was still off somewhere — she often hides and tries to pretend she had no part in things.

"*Hic!* It was a dare," Darby said. "I bet them — *hic!* — that I could do that."

"Why, Darby?" Lily asked. "You could have broken your neck."

Darby shrugged. For some strange reason, she seemed to be enjoying herself.

Mom ordered us to go find Dawn and head up to our room until she said we could leave. She needed to take headache medicine and figure out what to do with us.

"I've never been so disappointed in you girls in my life," she said.

It always makes us feel bad when she says that.

Dawn was already in our room when we got up there. We apologized to Darby and said we were glad she hadn't died. Then we bickered for a while about whose fault it was, until Darby said it didn't matter and that it was kind of fun anyway.

"Well, it was all for nothing," I grumbled. "Lily isn't inviting Alex, so we're back to square one."

"No, we aren't, because look what I managed to get," Dawn said with a sly smile. She reached underneath her pillow and pulled out an invitation. "Now *we* can invite him."

CHAPTER FOURTEEN

Uniform

Darby

I guess in hindsight it was a little thickheaded to eavesdrop that way, but tumbling off the roof was one of the most exciting things that ever happened to me. I can still remember lying there and listening as Lily and Burton suggested names and wrote them down — Burton pausing now and then to blow his nose. That part wasn't all that thrilling. But the next thing I knew, everything went herky-jerky, topsy-turvy, and soon I was flying through the air. Time seemed to stop and there was total silence. Just me and the breeze. Then I landed on the bush and heard Burton scream.

I keep trying to come up with a way to do it again. But I'll probably have to wait until the bush gets bushy once more, or I might break a bone.

Anyway, other than a slight rash on my arms, legs, and back of my neck, and a case of hiccups that took an hour to go away, I wasn't hurt. Mom sure was angry, though. She made me come downstairs while she called Dad to tell on me. After saying, "It's not funny!" over and over into the phone, she passed it to me. Dad told me to stop with all the hair-raising adventures before I put me or the rest of the family in the hospital. He said next time I wanted to go thrill-seeking, to let him know so he could find someplace with a safety net. I headed back upstairs wondering where Dad would find a net, and what sorts of daredevil stunts I could do to land in one. It sure sounded better than a prickly bush.

When I got back to the Triangular Office, Dawn had already filled out the invitation for Alex in her neat cursive writing. She had made sure to nab a copy with the extra insert invite to the rehearsal dinner, so we checked that it was in there, along with the RSVP card and envelope, before we sealed it shut. "See?" I said as I put a stamp in the upper corner. "This was all worth it."

The next day, we put Operation Post Office in motion. This plan required no derring-do or antics. Basically, we went downstairs and told Mom how extra sorry we were for the commotion. Mom looked as if she didn't believe us, but when we offered to do extra cleanup chores as penance, she took us up on it.

Here's a thing about being a triplet. As long as two of you are in sight, no one worries. If only one — or none — of you can be seen, parents start freaking out. So while Dawn and I swept up the althea bush mess and weeded the front flower beds, Delaney was able to sneak away and run to the post office. She's the fastest runner of all of us, so it made sense for her to go and do it. Dawn and I made sure to stay in motion and switch places now and then, to make it seem more like three of us instead of two. And after about thirty minutes, Delaney was back.

"I did it!" she said, all sweaty and panting and grinning with victory. And we took a break long enough to whoop and turn cartwheels.

"Now Alex will know Lily still likes him!" Dawn said.

"Maybe he'll come over now!" Delaney said.

"Maybe he'll show up with flowers and tell her to marry him instead of Burton!" I said.

We were whirling about and singing a song we made up called "Bye-Bye, Burton," when Mrs. Caldwell's big gold-colored car pulled up in the driveway. Three girls were with her. Two of them looked a lot alike. They were both skinny and had brown hair and pouty faces. The third girl had dyed black hair and so much makeup, it was hard to tell her expression. She was wearing a short black dress with ripped stockings and black boots.

"Is she a pirate?" Delaney asked. We knew she was talking about the girl in all black.

"Maybe a vampire," Dawn suggested.

"She reminds me of a raccoon," I said, noticing the dark lines around her eyes.

As they walked toward us and the house, I heard one of the pouty girls say to Mrs. Caldwell, "Are those the little brats?" But I couldn't hear Mrs. Caldwell's reply.

"Good morning, girls," Mrs. Caldwell said once they were right in front of us. "I'd like you to meet my nieces, Mavis and Felicia." She gestured to the pouty girls. They looked so much alike, I'd originally wondered if they were twins, but they weren't. Felicia was taller and obviously the older one, perhaps seventeen years old or so, and Mavis was probably around fifteen. "And this is Bree, Burton's other cousin on his father's side," she said, with a lazy wave toward the pirate girl.

"Hi," we said.

None of them said hi back. It was hard to tell who was the least happy to be there. The pouty girls were huffing and sighing and staring at the sky. The other girl looked like she'd dressed for a funeral, and had the expression to match. And Mrs. Caldwell seemed extra twitchy around us — probably due to the shenanigans the day before.

Dawn, Delaney, and I weren't exactly turning flips over their arrival either. In fact, we had been skipping about and celebrating but stopped when they got there.

We heard the door open and Lily came down the walkway toward us.

"Are you ready?" Mrs. Caldwell asked.

"Where are you going?" Delaney asked.

Mrs. Caldwell answered before Lily had a chance. "Your sister is coming with us to a nice shop where we'll pick out dresses for her bridesmaids."

"Oh," Delaney said. "Who are the bridesmaids?"

Felicia made a huffy noise. "We are. Duh."

"Dawn, Darby, and Delaney should come, too," Lily said. "After all, they're the flower girls."

Mrs. Caldwell made a shuddery sort of movement. "That isn't really necessary," she said. "We could pick out something for them. Besides, I can't fit everyone in my car."

"I can take them in my car," Lily said. "And it will be so much easier if they can try things on. We don't have time for anything to hold up the wedding."

At this, Mrs. Caldwell seemed to change her mind. I looked over at Dawn and Delaney. None of us wanted to go, but it was nice to see Lily have her way for a change.

We invited Mom to come, too, but she was on a deadline. She warned us about a trillion times to behave or else, and Lily promised to keep a close eye on us. Then we all piled into Lily's car and followed Mrs. Caldwell. On the way, we asked Lily why Clare, her best friend, wouldn't be a bridesmaid, and Lily explained that Clare was studying in Ireland and couldn't make it back in time. When Dawn started complaining about how Burton's family was taking over the wedding, Lily pointed out that we got to be flower girls and that it was nice that Burton's cousins got to participate.

Then we were there. We pulled up at a swanky boutique called Amelia's that I'd never noticed before, even though it was just a couple of doors down from Reinheimer's, a barbecue place that Dad always takes us to.

Inside, we were helped by a woman with a bun so tight it stretched her face. It hurt to look at her. At first, she ignored us and started pulling out dresses for the bridesmaids. Felicia immediately fell in love with a lacy lilac-colored one with a long skirt, and Mavis gushed over one in bright, shiny, peach-colored fabric that had a short skirt. After they tried them on, they started arguing over which one was better. It was odd seeing girls in fancy dresses call each other names like "stink breath."

Since they were so caught up in their disagreement, the lady with the bun started helping us.

"What are you doing in the wedding?" she asked.

"We're the fake flower girls," Delaney replied.

The woman looked confused until Dawn explained that the flowers were fake, not us.

After that, she started pulling out dresses from every part of the store to show us. Each gown was very different, but they were all horrible. One was gossamer-looking, as if it were made out of tissue paper. The other had so many sparkles, it seemed like something a fairy would wear. Delaney must have had the same thought, because she asked if it came with wings. Another dress had multicolored flowers sewn onto the top, and the skirt was made out of three big ruffles. "I just can't," Dawn said. "I'd feel like a walking wedding cake."

Finally, the lady gave up and suggested to Lily and Mrs. Caldwell that we look around on our own. This made us feel better until Mrs. Caldwell started showing us dresses that we liked even less — each one more poufy or ruffly or sequin-y than the one before it.

"Maybe we should go with the giant cake dress," I mumbled when Mrs. Caldwell swept off to find something else. "Her choices are worse."

Dawn snorted angrily. "Well, what did you expect? Her old dress, the one Lily is borrowing, has big marshmallow sleeves and a skirt as wide as Houston."

"Has she even seen us?" Delany said. "I mean we never wear dresses. Never. What makes her think we'll go all princess now?"

Lily managed to find a simpler one, but it was so hot pink, it hurt our eyes.

"It's very fancy here. There just isn't anything that fits your taste," Lily said.

Mrs. Caldwell returned, holding up a dress with a long, tight, scalloped skirt — like a mermaid. When we told her we'd trip and fall in it, she threw back her head, said, "I give up!" to the ceiling, and stalked to the other side of the store.

Lily sighed. "I'll go talk to her. You all look around. But be careful, okay? Please — no stunts."

I looked at our reflection in the nearby mirror. The three of us looked as pouty as Mavis and Felicia.

"I hate to say it," I said. "But I'd rather be home doing yard work."

"I'm going to the bathroom," Delaney said.

"I'm going outside to breathe in the barbecue," Dawn said.

I wasn't sure what to do, so I just stood there amid the sparkly dresses, listening to Mavis and Felicia sniping at each other. I sort of felt like hiding inside one of the dress racks, the way I used to do when I was younger, but I was too big to do that anymore. Instead, I walked up real close to the mirror and yanked at the hair on either side of my face until my features went all flat and stretched like the bun lady's.

I didn't want to be there. I didn't want to be with most of those people. And I didn't want Lily to be getting married in the first place.

Why did people have weddings anyway? I thought they were supposed to be wonderful, but so far, there didn't seem to be any part of it that was fun. Ugly dresses and rings. Stressed-out people. Lots of work. There was cake, and that was usually a good thing, but why not just have dessert, say "I do," and forget everything else?

"I hate this place," I mumbled to my stretchy reflection.

"I hate it, too," I heard someone say — only, it wasn't Dawn or Delaney. I turned around and saw Bree standing there. She was wearing a pink dress that I'd seen the bun lady give her earlier. And, well, there's just no way to put it nicely. She looked ridiculous. She was so pale, the color was extra loud on her. So instead of cotton candy or a carnation or the soft colors of sunset, it reminded me of . . . a slice of ham.

"Oh, hi. You look . . . you look . . ." I wanted to say something nice but couldn't think of anything and started stammering. I hate being shy.

"I look like a naked mole rat," she grumbled as she stepped up to the mirror and turned from side to side.

I tried not to laugh. I had no idea what a naked mole rat looked like, but it was probably true.

"My mom owes me big-time for making me do this," she said. Then she spun around and gave me what might have been a smile, except I couldn't tell, with all her raccoon makeup. "Excuse me," she said. "I have to go change before I puke."

Again I just stood there like a dummy as she walked off. I was amazed that we triplets weren't the only ones who thought this whole dress-up part was stupid. Of course, I was also amazed that a girl who dressed like a vampire pirate couldn't get into the spirit of a wedding costume.

And then, right at that moment, I saw it. On a rack in the far corner of the store. The perfect outfit!

I grabbed it and headed toward Delaney, who was just

coming back from the bathroom. On my way, I poked my head outside to tell Dawn to come back in.

"Look," I said, holding up the outfit as we all gathered around.

"It's perfect," Dawn said.

"Yes! I would wear that!" Delaney said, hopping up and down.

We took it over to Lily and Mrs. Caldwell.

"We want to wear this," I said, lifting it up.

"A tuxedo?" Mrs. Caldwell said.

Lily smiled really big. "I love it!"

"But those are for ring bearers, not flower girls," Mrs. Caldwell said.

Then Lily did something I'd never seen her do before. She lifted her chin the same way Mom does when she's quietly mad and said, "I don't care. They are doing this as a favor for me, so they should be able to wear whatever they wish."

Dawn, Delaney, and I looked at each other. I'm sure I had on the same expression they did: astonished and proud at the same time.

"In fact, I think everyone in the wedding party should wear what they want," Lily went on. She called out to Felicia and Mavis — who were still bickering — and then to Bree. "I've decided that instead of choosing one dress design, I'm going to let everyone wear what they want," she told them. "So choose whatever you like."

The sisters gaped at her.

"Are you kidding me?" Bree said.

"No, I'm serious."

"But then they won't match!" Mrs. Caldwell said. She seemed all in a dither. Her eyes were big and her movements were jerky. Again I was reminded of a spooked deer.

"Who cares?" Lily said. "This is my wedding and I want everyone to be comfortable."

"So I can get this?" Felicia said, holding up the lilac dress.

"And I can get this?" Mavis said, holding up the peachy one.

"Yep," Lily said with a grin.

"Best. Bride. Ever," Bree said.

Mrs. Caldwell threw up her hands. "Well! I can tell I'm not needed here." She marched over to a chair by the dressing room and started flipping noisily through a magazine.

Everyone — except Mrs. Caldwell — left the store happy that day. Mavis and Felicia stopped fighting because they each got the dress they wanted. Bree found a bright red dress that she could wear with her boots.

The three of us ordered white tuxedoes — mine with a white bow tie, Dawn's with a red one, and Delaney's with a blue one. And the bun lady seemed happy to see us go. It was satisfaction all around.

And that, I thought, should be what weddings are about.

CHAPTER FIFTEEN

Gross Domestic Product

Dawn

Unfortunately, Mrs. Caldwell didn't share Darby's opinion. She seemed to think weddings were all about stressing out as many people as possible.

"Mrs. Caldwell is coming over with a can of paste," I heard Darby say the next morning. I heard her, but I didn't really do anything because I was still asleep and I figured I must be having a weird dream.

Delaney is almost always the first triplet who wakes up, which is a good arrangement. She's a morning person and usually goes and gets some wiggles out of her system by playing with Quincy in the yard. Then, by the time she's ready for cereal, we're up. But some days, she gets bored and lonely and wakes us on purpose — although she won't admit it.

Wham!

I sat up in bed, startled and blinking. Across the room, I could see Darby doing the same thing.

"Sorry," Delaney said. "I accidentally knocked over that book."

My big heavy biography of Abraham Lincoln was lying on the floor about four feet away — which meant Delaney probably tossed it instead of knocked it.

Before I could complain, Delaney said again, "Hey, guys. Mrs. Caldwell is coming over with a can of paste that she wants us to try."

This time, I really listened to the words. "Huh?" I said.

"Why? I don't need to glue anything," Darby said. "Did you break something with all your bouncing, Delaney?"

"No, I didn't. I swear," Delaney said. "Apparently, Mrs. Caldwell is bringing the paste at lunchtime. Mom has to meet with a client and might be late. She wants us to eat breakfast and do our household tasks before Mrs. Caldwell gets here. She left instructions downstairs."

I groaned and threw the bedsheet over me. Mom also didn't agree with Darby's definition of weddings. She seemed to think they were all about chores.

Mom was still trying to get the house super tidy and sparkling for the wedding, so she had a new list of things she wanted us to clean — including stuff we've never cleaned before, like doorframes and windowsills and the screen door. You'd be surprised at the gunk that can build up on a thin strip of wood. Darby wanted to make a collection of all the dead bugs we found, but we talked her out of it.

While we did all that, Lily polished Mom's silver and washed her china sets so they could be used for serving food at the reception. I had to admit, the house had never looked so good — at least, not as far as I could remember. I found myself stopping and admiring each of the downstairs rooms as I stepped into them. Even Quincy kept sniffing everything as if he thought he was in a brand-new place.

Around noon, we heard the crunch of gravel outside. I peeked through the living room window and saw Mrs. Caldwell coming up the porch steps with a stack of white to-go boxes.

Delaney opened the door. "Did you bring the paste?" she asked.

"Paste?" Mrs. Caldwell looked confused. "Why would I bring paste?"

Delaney shrugged. "Mom said you were bringing over a can of paste for us to try. Only, I don't know why. I didn't break anything recently — I promise."

"Oh. I think you mean *canapés*," Lily said, putting her hand on Delaney's shoulder. "It does sound like 'can of paste.' It's a type of appetizer, and she's bringing samples for us to try. To serve at the wedding."

"Can of paste! Oh ho ho! Can of paste." Mrs. Caldwell kept shaking her head and making that chirruping laugh of hers as she headed into the dining room.

Delaney ducked her head slightly. Her cheeks looked as if they'd been roasted.

It was kind of funny, but I didn't laugh. Instead, I felt bad for my sister.

"Don't worry about it, Delaney," I whispered, patting her other shoulder. "She's just a big meanie."

"Yeah," Darby said. "And, hey. At least she's not accusing you of breaking something."

Lily followed Mrs. Caldwell into the dining room, with us close behind. Mrs. Caldwell had already set down her packages and was standing at the head of the table as if she were in charge of everything in the world.

"Now, before we get to the tasting, I have big news to share." Mrs. Caldwell had her hands pressed together and was bouncing slightly in her pointy shoes. It looked like she was doing a bad impression of Delaney. "The reporter who writes the society column for the paper will be coming to the rehearsal dinner!"

For a few seconds, no one made a sound. Eventually, I said, "Why?"

Mrs. Caldwell's smile fell away. "Because Burton's marriage is big news. It has to be covered. In fact, I wouldn't be surprised if they do a huge write-up on it."

"Oh my," said Lily. "Well, how about that?" She seemed to be doing a bad impression of an excited person. "So! How about we sample the food before it gets cold?"

We all stood around as Mrs. Caldwell opened each of the six boxes, one by one. "I have food samples from five nearby caterers, along with some booklets that list what they offer," she said, setting down the books. "I'll help you decide on the menu so you can place the order sometime today."

I hated the way Mrs. Caldwell was bossing people — especially Lily. At the same time, I was curious, so I stepped forward and peered into the boxes. Each one held some sort of colorful bite-size food.

"Don't they all look delicious?" Mrs. Caldwell said.

"They all look meaty," Delaney said.

I looked over the selection again, and it was true. Each one was full of beef or wrapped in bacon or topped with fish.

"Lily can't eat any of this," Darby said. "She's vegetarian."

Mrs. Caldwell either didn't hear her or pretended not to. Instead, she bit into a meatball and went "*Mmmm*."

"It's okay," Lily said to Darby. "I'm sure I can find some good options in these books. You girls go ahead and try them. It's lunchtime after all."

"But what about you?" Delaney asked.

"I'll make myself a sandwich later."

The appetizers were all right, but I felt bad eating them. Also, the meatballs were gross. They were slimy and dog-food-ish. I wouldn't even give them to Quincy.

Meanwhile, Lily sat down at the table and flipped through catering booklets while we stood eating and looking over her shoulder.

Some of the options, like the fruit and vegetable trays, were pretty typical and boring, but others were kind of creative. Like the place that would carve the names of the bride and groom into a watermelon. Or the cake balls on sticks that were decorated and tied with ribbons to resemble bouquets of flowers.

One restaurant even had photos of mashed potato sculptures they could make for a wedding. These included hearts, doves, swans, and wedding rings — the nice kind that didn't look like toilet seats.

"They forgot the arms on this lady," I said, looking at an image of a woman's head and torso shaped from mashed potatoes and sitting on a bed of parsley.

Lily glanced at the photo. "That's a replica of the Venus de Milo, a famous statue by a brilliant artist. She doesn't have arms."

"I don't get it," Delaney whispered to me. "If the artist is so great, why would he forget the arms?"

I shrugged.

"Oh, these are amazing," Mrs. Caldwell said as she munched on some cheesy thing with bacon. "Burton will love these."

Lily's forehead went squiggly. "Excuse me. I'm going to go make a peanut butter sandwich," she said. Then she stood and headed into the kitchen.

Darby, Delaney, and I exchanged guilty looks. No way could we eat another meaty bite after that. Instead, we sat at the table and started flipping through the catering books.

"This place says you can choose four kinds of . . . horse doves," Darby said excitedly. "What are those? Do they fly?"

"What?" Mrs. Caldwell sounded startled. She peered over Darby's shoulder. "Those are hors d'oeuvres. They're appetizers — like canapés."

"Why do they give wedding food such strange names?" Delaney asked.

"Yeah, like these teeny-tiny burgers," I said. "Why are they called *sliders*?"

"My, my," Mrs. Caldwell said. "You girls certainly ask a lot of questions."

I waited to see if she would give me a real answer, but she didn't.

"Well, then," said Mrs. Caldwell, dabbing at the corners of her mouth with a napkin. "I think it's obvious that these meatballs would be best, along with some salmon-topped canapés and bacon sliders."

"But . . . Lily doesn't eat meat. She's vegetarian," Darby said, louder and more slowly than when she said it before.

"Yes, but Lily isn't going to be the only person eating at the wedding," Mrs. Caldwell said.

"Yes, but Lily is the bride," Delaney said.

"Yes, but this wedding also includes a big strong boy who needs nourishment," Mrs. Caldwell said.

Darby, Delaney, and I exchanged puzzled looks. "What big strong boy?" I asked.

"Why, Burton, of course."

"Yes, but this is Lily's house, and she needs nourishment, too," I pointed out, my voice rising a little. "Burton can eat vegetables, but she can't eat meat."

"Yes, but the meat eaters who will be attending the wedding will far outnumber the vegetarians."

"Yes, but since Lily's parents are actually paying for the food, it seems only fair that they have the final decision about what is served. Don't you agree, Edith?" Mom was standing in the doorway to the dining room, still holding her car keys. She must have just returned from her appointment and we hadn't heard her because we'd been busy bickering.

At this point, Mrs. Caldwell seemed to run out of *yes buts*. "Well, I . . . I . . ." She twitched and sputtered like a dying campfire. "Of course, Anne. If you want to disappoint the multitude of guests, there is nothing I can do about it. However, you should be aware that I plan to serve meat as the main course at the rehearsal dinner. And that will be paid for by me."

"That sounds fair," Lily said, entering the dining room from the kitchen.

"No, it's not," I said. "You won't be able to eat hardly anything and you're the bride!"

"I'm sure I will find things I can eat, Dawn. It's okay. And, as I said, it's fair."

"Since my input isn't appreciated here, I believe I'll go finalize the menu for the rehearsal dinner," Mrs. Caldwell said. She stuck her nose in the air and trotted toward the front door.

"Thank you for bringing over the booklets and samples," Lily said, going after her.

Mom sat down and sighed. She had a headachy look on her face.

"Mom, why do wedding plans make people crazy?" Darby asked.

"It's not the plans that do it," she said. "It's the emotions. This is a big thing happening to people we love. Mrs. Caldwell wants what she thinks is best for Burton, because she loves him — just like we love Lily and want what's best for her. Mrs. Caldwell is just a little more . . . forceful about saying what she wants."

"Well, we outnumber her. So there," I said.

Mom laughed. "Yes, I suppose we do."

When Lily got back to the dining room, the five Brewster women sat around with the catering books and discussed the menu for the wedding reception. After some civilized debate, we finally decided on the following: Spinach and goat cheese mini quiches, stuffed mushrooms, watercress canapés topped with assorted vegetables, and the vegetarian sliders. I thought the menu was quite representative of us Brewsters — it was good and real, without any fancy, showy stuff.

But the absolute best part of the day was when Lily let me, Darby, and Delaney flip through the books and pick out the wedding cake. We easily agreed on it. We chose a three-tiered one that had vanilla on the bottom, chocolate in the middle, and strawberry on top. There were multicolored frosting flowers all along the bottom, and candy rainbows around the middle — and piles and piles of whipped white frosting that made it look like a big cloud was sitting on top. We figured if Lily couldn't be outdoors for her wedding, even though she'd always wanted to be, we could bring the outdoors to her in this small way.

It felt good to truly help and not just pretend. The only thing that would have made it even better was if Lily had let us help choose her groom.

CHAPTER SIXTEEN

High Alert

Delaney

Wedding RSVP cards arrived in the mail nearly every day, but there was never one from Alex. Dawn, Darby, and I despaired over this every evening. We began to wonder if we had sent it to the wrong place or if he wasn't going to come — or hadn't decided yet. Of course, we also knew that if Lily saw it, there would be lots of questions, but we preferred having to endure that to Alex being left out entirely.

Truth was, we were beginning to give up hope. Time was running out and there was nothing we could do to prevent the wedding day from arriving. Dawn kept calling meetings where we would sit around and complain and not come up with any good ideas. Darby kept getting the hiccups. And I got so jittery and fidgety that I would knock stuff over without meaning to. Our extra-clean living and dining rooms were in danger of getting messy again, so Mom actually stopped making me clear the table. I had to fold towels instead.

It was shaping up to be the most worrisome summer vacation ever. Romping in the Neighbors' sprinklers didn't even feel fun anymore. Outings with Daddy for pizza or ice cream didn't cheer us up. Even trips to Forever's for pie didn't help.

One morning, Mom came upstairs and told us to clean our room. "And I mean really clean it," she said. "Do not just toss things under the beds or into the closet. I will be checking those places, too, to make sure they are clean and tidy."

"But that will take forever!" Dawn whined.

"Then you better start now," Mom said. "Lily is out with your father, and I need to go pick up Aunt Jane at the airport. I expect this place to be spick-and-span or on its way to a high state of cleanliness by the time we get back. If you need anything, ask Ms. Woolcott."

We grumbled for about an hour after she left and then spent close to another hour coming up with a plan. We decided that I should tidy the closet since I'm one-eighth of an inch taller than the others and can reach the shelves better. Meanwhile, Darby would clean under my bed and hers, and Dawn would clean under her bed, sweep the floor, and take out the trash.

The closet door never can stay open for some reason. Sure enough, it swung shut as soon as I stepped in there.

I was feeling around in the air for the pull string to turn on the light, when I heard a noise. It was low and whirring — like a growly animal or a buzzing insect. *Whuzzz whuzzz whuzzz.*

"Quincy?" I said. Only, I knew he wasn't up there.

And that's when I saw them. Three sets of evil, glowing, yellow eyes staring right at me in the dark.

One of my talents is that I can scream intolerably loud, and I think I screamed the loudest ever at that moment. I didn't know if the ghost had moved upstairs and invited over some friends, or rabid raccoons had set up house in our closet, or a bunch of vampire bats had mistaken it for their cave. All I knew was that I was about to get eaten.

I tried to get out of there, but because it was messy, I kept tripping over stuff. Eventually, I found the knob and burst through the door to find Darby and Dawn looking panicked. Dawn was already standing on her bed.

"Eyes!" I shouted and then tore out of the room and down the stairs. They followed close behind. Quincy, who must have heard the scream, joined up with us and went straight for his kennel.

I didn't stop until I made it to the middle of the front yard. I leaned against the flagpole to catch my breath.

"What in tarnation, Delaney?" Dawn asked. "What do you mean 'eyes'?"

I described to them what I'd seen and heard.

"Locusts?" Dawn asked.

"Nope. No way. Those eyes weren't buglike. They were more like an ogre's or a troll's. Or a . . . a . . . chupacabra's!"

"So the eyes were really big?" Darby asked.

I thought for a second. "No, kind of small. But not as small as bug eyes."

"I wonder . . ." Darby said, tapping her chin. Then she turned and headed for the house, saying, "I'm going to check something. Dawn, you can come, too."

I stayed put as the two of them went back inside. Even though I was standing still, my heart was galloping as if it wanted to bust out of me and keep racing down the street. I was worried about my sisters. And I was worried about the future. Now that our house was infested with hobgoblins, where would I sleep?

A couple of minutes later, Darby and Dawn came back out. They were smiling and chuckling.

"What's so funny?" I asked

"This is what you were afraid of," Darby said. From behind her back, she produced a long box with three plastic kittens inside — the Sparkle Cats that Burton had given us. Dawn pointed to the sticker that mentioned they were glow-in-the-dark and had motion-sensor purring sounds. I'd forgotten all about that stupid present.

"Well, gee," I said, feeling foolish. "They look a lot less cute in the dark. Trust me."

"*Yoo-hoo!*"

We glanced up and saw Ms. Woolcott waving frantically from her side of the fence. The three of us walked over to see what was up.

"Is everything okay?" she asked. "I heard a blood-curdling scream. Should I call for help?"

"No, ma'am," I said. "We're fine. The scream came from me. I was just . . . I saw . . . I mean, I thought I saw . . ." It was one of those rare times when I was at a loss for words.

"We were just playing," Dawn said.

"I'm glad everyone is all right, but you girls gave me such a fright! I do believe my hair is sticking straight up."

Actually, Ms. Woolcott's hair always sticks up a couple of inches from her scalp, but we didn't want to argue with her.

"By the way, I've been meaning to stop by," Ms. Woolcott went on. "A piece of your mail was accidentally delivered to my house." She reached into the pocket of her skirt and pulled out a small envelope. "It looks like one of those RSVP cards from your sister's wedding invitation."

She held it up to show us, and I plucked it from her hands. The return label read A. HAWTHORNE and I recognized Alex's address. Immediately, I started bouncing on my toes. Dawn and Darby noticed and let out little whoops.

"Oh? Is it a good one?" asked Ms. Woolcott in her singsongy voice.

"Not really," I said, trying to throw off her nosy nose. "We're just excited whenever we get one. It's like a game."

"You girls sure do play a lot of games," Ms. Woolcott said. "Stick with the quiet ones today, all right? The ones with no screaming?" She patted her hairdo, but each time she pressed down, it boinged back up again.

"Yes, ma'am," I said. "Thank you, Ms. Woolcott."

We ran inside the house. As soon as I was through the front door, I opened the envelope and pulled out the card. Again my heart was scampering around inside me, and my fingers shook a little.

The little square next to ACCEPTS WITH PLEASURE had been checked.

"He's coming!" I shouted, bouncing around in a circle. It was the most beautiful card I'd ever seen — even if it was the color of a rain cloud and the writing was too curly. "He's really coming!" I was so happy I wanted to scream, but I didn't want Ms. Woolcott to call the sheriff's department again.

Dawn grabbed the card from me and did her own dance before passing it to Darby.

"So now what?" Darby asked, staring down at it.

"What do you mean 'now what'?" I said. "Now Lily and Alex will see each other and fall back in love."

"Are you sure?" she asked. "I mean, what if they don't? Is there anything else we can do?"

"Just wait and see, I guess," I said. Everyone had stopped celebrating and that annoyed me. I didn't want to stop bouncing and being happy.

"I don't want to wait," Dawn said. "I want to make sure they get back together. Or at least make sure she doesn't marry Burton."

"But this is the only one of our plans that actually worked," I said. "Face it — we're kind of lousy at stopping weddings."

Dawn tapped her chin the way she always does when she's pondering hard. "There's got to be something we can do."

She didn't get to think about it for long, though. Because just then the door opened and Aunt Jane walked in.

CHAPTER SEVENTEEN

Allies

Dawn

Triplets! Come huddle up!" Aunt Jane shouted.

Aunt Jane is one of our favorite people in the whole history of people. She's tall and strong. She played professional basketball for a while and then taught PE classes here in Blanco County. Now she lives in Boston, where she runs a bar.

That's another thing we like about Aunt Jane — she's tough. Mom says she's seen her step in between men fighting each other and toss them out of her establishment. We hope to go visit her, and she always says she can't wait to take us to see the famous sites in her adopted city. Mom is still wondering if that's a good idea, though. She says that, on one hand, Aunt Jane is probably the only person who can truly handle us, but on the other hand, we probably inherited our penchant for foolishness from her, and the four of us set loose might cause a national crisis.

So as soon as we saw Aunt Jane's short, curly hair and big smile, we shouted hoorays and ran over to hug her. Quincy, too. He finally came out of his kennel and kept rising up on his hind legs and doing a little happy dance. Aunt Jane gave us Quincy when he was a puppy, right before she moved to Boston, and I don't think he ever forgot that. Mom never has, either. She mentions Aunt Jane whenever Quincy does something bad.

Aunt Jane suggested we all go run and play, but then Mom asked if we'd finished cleaning our room.

"Almost," I said, but she just ignored me.

"Darby?" Mom tends to focus on Darby whenever she wants the truth. That's because she's the lousiest liar. "How much is left to do?"

"Oh . . . maybe just . . . most of it," she said, hanging her head a little. I couldn't tell if she was ashamed that our chore wasn't finished or that she was no good at lying.

But just as we were about to go upstairs and clean, Aunt Jane convinced Mom to reconsider. She said that it was already hot and would only get hotter. She said she hadn't seen us in way too long. And she said, besides, she was older and tougher and should get her way. (She said that last part with a grin.) Mom gave in (also with a grin) but made us promise to finish cleaning the minute we came back inside.

Like I said, Aunt Jane is just about the best there is.

We headed outside to our hill. For a while, we played Frisbee and tossed a stick for Quincy until he decided he'd rather gnaw on it than bring it back to us. Then we all sat cross-legged under the red oak.

"You girls are growing up so fast," Aunt Jane said, shaking her head. "I can't believe our Lily is getting married."

"Yeah," Delaney said, her face all weighed down. "Neither can we."

"Ah." Aunt Jane raised her left eyebrow. "I take it you aren't too happy about it?"

For a few seconds, we just sat there, exchanging glances. And then suddenly, Darby said, "Burton's a nincompoop!"

After that, we all started grumbling at once. We told Aunt Jane about Mrs. Caldwell's takeover of the wedding plans and Burton spending more time holding his book bag than Lily's hand and the squiggly lines on Lily's forehead and how everyone's stress level had reached the rings of Saturn at this point.

When we finished, Aunt Jane looked all glowery.

"We know, we know," I said. "We need to respect Lily's decision and give Burton a chance."

"A chance? Ha! I've known Burton Caldwell since he was a sniveling first grader, and I agree that he is not a man who can make Lily happy."

I was so surprised to hear this, I almost toppled over onto the grass. Darby and Delaney also seemed light-headed with surprise.

"What happened to that nice fellow Alex?" Aunt Jane asked.

"They broke up," Darby said. "We don't know why."

Aunt Jane made a little grunting noise that sounded like *gah*. "That's too bad. He and Lily seemed perfect for each other."

We nodded. I saw Delaney pat the pocket where she'd stuck Alex's RSVP.

"I don't understand why Lily is in such a hurry to get married," Aunt Jane said. "She's still so young. And marriage isn't something to rush into. It's something you should take a long time to decide about."

"Is that why you haven't gotten married yet?" Delaney asked. Darby and I gave her warning looks. That girl is always asking too many personal questions.

"Child, I don't even want to share my life with a cat,"

Aunt Jane said, chuckling. "I like to do things my way all the time. Marriage isn't for everyone."

At that point, it was really hot, and we were all squished together in a small patch of shade, so we agreed we should go back inside.

Knowing we had more time with Aunt Jane to look forward to made us clean our room extra fast. When we were done, we came downstairs and found Mom and Aunt Jane giggling. The big box of photos was down from the top of the closet, and the coffee table was covered with old pictures. Mom always laughs more when her sister is around. Once Aunt Jane got her laughing so hard, she spit water all over her. It was amazing. The wall behind Aunt Jane was covered with drops except for a dry spot in the shape of her head. We were hoping it would stay that way forever, but Mom cleaned it up.

Delaney had just asked if she could get the two of them some ice water — I could tell she was hoping to see Mom spray the wall again — when the door opened and Dad and Lily came in.

"Jane!" Dad said.

Aunt Jane leaped up from her chair and they did that thing they always do where they pretend to have a boxing match and end up hugging.

Meanwhile, Mom sat there and shook her head at them. She always said Daddy acted more like Aunt Jane's sibling than she did. Aunt Jane likes to say Mom was born a boring grown-up and that she was never real good at clowning around.

"How are you, Phil-dog?" Aunt Jane asked Daddy.

"Mean and ornery as ever," he replied. "You?"

"You know me. Busier than a one-legged man in a butt-kicking contest."

"Well, we're glad you're kicking around here."

"Hi, Aunt Jane," Lily said, stepping forward.

Aunt Jane gathered her up in a big hug and then pulled back and frowned at her. "Miss Lily, what's happened to your sparkle? Nothing can take the pretty out of you, but I've never seen your face so puckered and dull."

"I've just been under a lot of stress with the wedding plans and all," Lily said, staring down at the floor.

"Nonsense. You're a bride-to-be. Shouldn't you be extra radiant?"

"Well . . . it's been more stressful than most, I think. There hasn't been a lot of time to plan."

Aunt Jane shook her head slowly and sat back down.

"Oh! That reminds me." Lily dug through her purse and pulled out a flash drive. "I have a surprise for all of you."

"What is it?" Mom asked.

"Burton's family made a slide show to be played at the rehearsal dinner."

"I want to see it!" Delaney said.

Lily smiled. "I thought you might."

She put it into Mom's computer and we all gathered around to watch. I wasn't sure what it would be like, but even though I didn't have any expectations, I was still disappointed. It started with the photo of Lily and Burton — the one Mrs. Caldwell gave Mom as a gift — but then the whole rest of it was picture after picture of Burton. Poor guy looked even more like an armadillo when he was young. And I guess he's always had that same expression on his face, all stiff and uncomfortable — as if he were being pinched from behind. Delaney wondered aloud if he looked that way even when he slept, but Mom shushed her.

All through the show, this song kept playing, where a woman kept talking about heroes and wind and wings. Apparently, I wasn't the only one who didn't understand why they picked it, because at one point, Aunt Jane said, "How come they chose old-lady funeral music?"

Eventually, it was over. Nobody seemed to have anything to say about it. Then Delaney said, "Where the heck was Lily? How come Lily isn't in there?"

"They were in a hurry," Lily said. "And it's not like they have a lot of photos of me."

"Only one of you and Burton together? That's all?" asked Dad.

"It's your wedding, too," I said. "You should be in there."

"Maybe we can add some of ours," Mom suggested.

Lily shook her head. "I'm no good with tech stuff."

"We can do it. It's easy!" Darby said. "You're so busy anyway. Let me, Dawn, and Delaney help."

Lily took out the flash drive and looked at it. "Well, I don't know . . ."

"What's the harm?" Aunt Jane said. "Like you said, they would have included you if they'd had photos of you. This way we save them the trouble."

"You guys would do that for me?" Lily asked, looking at Darby.

"Of course!" Darby said. "We can even make the music better."

Lily thanked her about six times and handed over the flash drive. "I really appreciate this."

Darby turned to Mom. "Can we use the box of old photos? We want to include some old baby pictures of Lily."

Mom smiled at that idea. "Sure."

"Don't include my seventh-grade yearbook photo!" Lily said as Darby and I each grabbed an end of the box and started carrying it up the stairs.

"And make sure I have hair in all my shots!" Dad called out.

As soon as we got up to the Triangular Office, I shut the door and said, "Why on earth did you volunteer us for this, Darby? We need to be stopping the wedding, not helping with a stupid slide show."

"But we *are* helping to stop it," Darby said, her eyes all sparkly and sneaky-looking. "I have a plan."

CHAPTER EIGHTEEN

This Is Only a Drill

Darby

I was happy it was me who had the brilliant idea for once. Usually, it's Dawn who comes up with our strategies, followed by Delaney. Occasionally, I'll hatch a scheme, but it usually involves me jumping out of a tree or hanging from the roof. This was a relatively low risk and wholesome plan for me.

I shared my suggestion with everyone and they agreed it might work. We called it Operation Face-the-Facts. After brainstorming a few minutes, we headed back downstairs before anyone got suspicious.

Mom was holding the phone and a menu for Pie in the Sky. "I'm not cooking in my clean kitchen," she said. "So tell me what kind of pizza you want."

Dawn shouted, "Olive and mushroom!" and Delaney shouted, "Pepperoni!" I told her, anything but anchovies.

Dad got up from his chair and started for the door.

"Phil, you're staying for dinner, aren't you?" Aunt Jane asked.

"Well . . . I . . . um . . ." Daddy looked over at Mom.

Mom hesitated for a few seconds and then said, "Of course he's staying. This is the pre-rehearsal-dinner dinner. The whole family should be here."

Dawn and I looked at each other and grinned. Delaney bounced on her toes. She kept on bouncing in her chair as we ate pizza. And she boinged around the room afterward.

Aunt Jane made everything better.

After dinner, we worked on the slide show using our computer and scanner. We stayed up late finishing the presentation. When it was done, we were dog tired — even Quincy had gone to sleep ages ago — but we didn't want to go to bed. Because if we went to bed, we would wake up and it would be the next day — the day of the rehearsal and snooty dinner — just one day before the wedding.

"This is it. It's really happening, you guys," Dawn said. Her voice was all throaty like Quincy's gets when he whines.

"You mean it *might* happen," Delaney said. "It still might not. Alex is coming. And we have a good plan."

"If it does happen, I guess we'll be okay," I said. "This hasn't been all bad, you know. We get to see Aunt Jane. And Daddy is hanging around more. Still . . . I really really really hope the wedding doesn't happen."

"I'd even be happy if the rehearsal and rehearsal dinner didn't happen," Dawn grumbled.

"Yeah, what if our plan doesn't work?" I said.

"It's going to be awful," Delaney said. "And poor Lily! She probably won't even get to eat tomorrow because of all the meat Mrs. Caldwell is having them serve. She'll faint from lack of food — and she's the bride!"

Dawn made a growly kind of noise. "Ooh, it really steams me how Mrs. Caldwell has taken over everything. And you know what? I'm going to do something about it." She got up and headed out of our room and down the stairs. Delaney and I exchanged confused looks, and then a few seconds later, Dawn returned with the phone. "I'm calling the restaurant and changing the dinner menu," she said.

Delaney looked up the place on the Internet. "Hurry," she said. "They're about to close."

Dawn punched in the number and waited. Her face was a bunch of crisscrossed lines and her eyes were fierce. "Yes," she said eventually. "I need to talk to someone about changing the menu for tomorrow night's dinner."

Delaney and I had to put pillows over our mouths to keep from laughing. Dawn had made her voice sound sort of like Mrs. Caldwell's — high and squawky like an angry turkey.

"Yes, we need it to be all vegetarian dishes," Dawn went on. "No meat. . . . Yes. . . . That is fine. . . . That, too. . . . Thank you very much. I am going to tell everyone in the world how great you are. Good-bye." She hung up the phone and gave a satisfied nod.

Dawn tried to get me to return the phone, but I was still laughing too hard, and Delaney is too fidgety and would get caught, so Dawn had to do it. By the time she got back, the laughter had stopped, and all the nervousness was back inside my stomach.

The three of us climbed into our beds, but all we could do was toss and turn and make whimpering sounds. We wondered if this was how presidents felt before an election or a big battle. And we each described our nervousness. Dawn said it felt like a big bear claw was squeezing her stomach. Delaney said it felt like a swarm of grasshoppers were leaping around inside her. I said it felt like jumping on a trampoline in roller skates after you've eaten four hot dogs. (I know because I actually did that.)

We kept on whispering in the dark, and the next thing I knew, it was morning. My hair was a tangled mess because I hadn't brushed out my braid before bedtime. Dawn had fallen asleep while holding her George Washington figurine, and you could see the impression of his sword on her left cheek. Delaney was already up — or maybe she'd never actually gone to sleep — and was running around the front yard with Quincy.

It was a tornado of a day. Mom, Lily, and Aunt Jane were zipping back and forth so much downstairs, we went outside to join Delaney. When it got too hot, we holed up in the Triangular Office. Delaney's a restless person to begin with, and when she's anxious, she's like a squirrel that drank too much coffee. She drove us batty with her constant chatter and boinging and zipping about. She couldn't stop messing with things, and her bouncing kept knocking things over, so after a while, our room was a total wreck again. But just when Dawn suggested tossing her out the window, Mom hollered upstairs for us to shower and get dressed for the rehearsal.

By the time we walked into the living room, Mrs. Caldwell was already there, bossing people around.

"That woman is a thorn in my rump," Aunt Jane whispered. We nodded.

Felicia, Mavis, and Bree were sitting on the couch, each of them texting on a cell phone. And it was odd seeing Mom and Lily standing off in a corner, as if they felt awkward in their own living room.

"Where is Burton?" Mrs. Caldwell kept saying, pacing in a circle and raising her arms. "Where could he have gone?"

Lily just stood there and shrugged. Poor Lily. She's the opposite of Delaney. When she's nervous, she just turns the color of an apple blossom and goes really quiet.

When Dawn gave her the flash drive with the slide show on it, Lily looked at her without really seeing her and mumbled "thanks." Then she stood there for several minutes just holding it until Mom took it and put it in her purse.

Finally, Burton showed up. He was as rumpled-looking as ever, but this time in slightly nicer clothes. He apologized for being late and explained he was in the library.

"Today?" Mrs. Caldwell shrieked.

"Of course," he said. He seemed surprised at her anger. "I had to since I won't have much time tomorrow."

"What on earth are you saying? You won't have *any* time tomorrow! Because tomorrow is your *wedding day*!"

I thought flames might shoot out from the bottom of Mrs. Caldwell's shoes and send her rocketing through our ceiling. Even the bridesmaids looked up from their cell phones.

"Now, where is the father of the bride?" said Mrs. Caldwell, pacing again. "Where is he?"

"He'll be here any second," Mom said. Then she turned to me and whispered. "Go find your father!"

I was just about to go call him when I heard his Vespa outside. "He's here!" I said.

Mom and I met him at the door.

"Phil! You're wearing that?" Mom asked.

Daddy had on his rainbow suspenders and red bow tie.

"You said to dress up," he said.

"That's dressing up?"

"I thought the tux was just for tomorrow?"

Mom shook her head. "Never mind. Come in. We need to get the rehearsal started right now."

For the next twenty minutes, Mrs. Caldwell had us practice the wedding. It was really silly. Basically, we all took turns walking down the aisle. First Dawn, Delaney, and I went. Mom didn't want us to throw the actual fake flowers because she wanted to keep the house clean, so we just pretended to throw stuff. Mrs.

Caldwell kept saying we were throwing too many flowers — even though we weren't throwing any. So then we had to go back to the beginning and throw every four steps.

"One, two, three, *throw*! One, two, three, *throw*!" Mrs. Caldwell kept chanting.

I thought Dawn was going to karate-kick her.

Eventually, Mrs. Caldwell was satisfied. Only, then we had to stand next to the potted palm that was supposed to be Reverend Hoffmeyer for the rest of the rehearsal. We couldn't talk or sit down, and anytime Delaney started boinging or swiveling, Mrs. Caldwell would tell her to keep still.

After us came Bree, then Mavis, and then Felicia. They also had to walk down the aisle over and over because they wouldn't put down their cell phones or kept rolling their eyes. Bree had to do it four times because Mrs. Caldwell said the boots made her lurch like a sick pony.

Meanwhile, Dawn, Delaney, and I were getting super antsy. It was hard standing still and we were worried about Operation Face-the-Facts. The only thing that got us through it was Aunt Jane. She kept pretending to trip people with her foot and made faces at Mrs. Caldwell behind her back until Mom made her stop.

When Mrs. Caldwell said we were done and it was time to go to the restaurant to meet our special guests and the newspaper reporter, everyone cheered.

The three of us huddled up before leaving the house. "Well, here goes nothing," Dawn said.

CHAPTER NINETEEN

Operation Face-the-Facts

Delaney

The rehearsal dinner was at a ritzy place just outside town called Cypress Creek Inn. I'm not sure why it's called that. In historical novels, inns are places where travelers can rest their horses, have a pint of ale and some mutton stew, and take a room for the night. But there were no beds anywhere. And the menu didn't have mutton stew as far as I could tell. It just looked like your typical fancy restaurant with soft music, tablecloths, and tiny candles on every table.

"The wedding party should stay in the foyer," Mrs. Caldwell told us.

"I thought the party was inside," I said, pointing into the main dining room.

Mrs. Caldwell said, "No. What I mean is, the people

who are in the wedding need to stand out here and greet the guests. That means flower girls, too."

And here I'd thought we were done with all the standing around. I was feeling crazy restless, so I asked Dawn and Darby to cover for me. "If I don't get this energy out of me, I'll burst apart in a disgusting display," I explained.

"Fine," Dawn said. "Go run around. They probably won't notice if one of us is missing. But you owe us!"

I promised I'd give them a break, too, after I'd settled myself down. Then I sneaked back outside to look for a good spot to do cartwheels.

I wasn't the only one playing hooky. I skipped around the side of the building and found Bree leaning against the wall, shaking her cell phone.

"Is it at all possible that you might have a cell phone charger?" she asked me.

"Nope," I said, propping my left foot on the wall beside her. "Mom won't let us have cell phones. She says giving us phones would be like giving computers to crocodiles. One time, I borrowed Lily's phone and tried to play a game on it but ended up taking all of these pictures of my nose on accident. Apparently, I e-mailed one to her old boss and —"

"Kiddo. Please. Take a breath," she said. "Aunt Edith has me so stressed, I came out here to get some peace — and send out some epic complaints. Only, my stupid phone died and I can't get ahold of anyone."

"You can complain to me," I said, switching legs.

She made a sniffing sound. "What are you? Like . . . ten?"

"No way," I said, straightening up as high as I could without actually getting on my tiptoes. "I'm eleven."

She followed me with her raccoon eyes as I headed to a patch of grass and did some cartwheels and jumping jacks.

"What's up with you anyway? Too much sugar?"

"This is how I deal with stress," I said. At that point, my body was beginning to settle down. I was still jittery, but I no longer felt as if all that energy trapped inside me was going to build into a big volcanic kablooie.

Bree gave up on her phone and tossed it into a leather bag that looked like it was black with white polka dots — but as I walked up next to her, I could see the white dots were actually skulls.

"Why did you agree to be a bridesmaid anyway?" I asked. "You look so miserable."

"Because my mom made me and, like a moron, I

thought it would be no big deal. I didn't realize it was going to be the disaster of the century."

I tilted my head. "What do you mean?"

Bree made another snorting sound, and I wondered if maybe she had allergies like Burton. "Please," she said. "It's so obvious that these guys are about to make a dumb but legally binding mistake. If Burton and Lily want a happily-ever-after, they should call off the wedding, because they won't find it with each other." Her eyes met mine. "Sorry. I know she's your sister."

"Doesn't bother me," I said. "We don't even want Lily to marry your cousin." I put my hands on the ground and kicked up my legs until I was doing a handstand against the wall.

Bree leaned over to look me in my upside-down face. "You don't?"

"Nope," I said — only, it came out sounding like "dope" because I was straining to hold myself up. As soon as I felt my shirt about to come untucked, I flipped back down. "We want her to marry Alex."

"Who's Alex?"

"Lily's old boyfriend. You might get to see him tonight."

"He's coming?" Bree hadn't looked or sounded this much alive since I'd met her.

"We hope," I said. "Speaking of . . . I should go back in. I don't want to miss him."

Bree followed me back inside the restaurant.

"You owe us," Dawn muttered as she saw me come in.

"Sorry. The wiggles were at critical mass. I had to do something."

I joined them in line, but it wasn't much of a line anymore. People were standing around in clusters, talking, and there was very little movement. Dawn, being Dawn, was getting surly and kept complaining about the air being hot and stuffy and stinking of perfume. Darby, being Darby, was feeling shy and kept hiding behind Dawn. I was starting to feel antsy again and wondered if I could sneak out to do one more cartwheel.

Eventually, Mrs. Caldwell said that people could follow her into the dining room. "The bride and groom and their attendants will stay in here and continue to greet guests."

"Are we attendants?" I asked Bree.

She nodded and rolled her eyes. Then suddenly, her eyes got wide and a small smile crept across her face.

"Who's the hunk?" she asked.

I turned around and there was Alex standing just inside the door. I quickly nudged Dawn and Darby. We all smiled at him — Bree, too — but he walked right past us and looked at Lily.

"Hi, Lily," he said.

Lily turned. As soon as she saw him, she turned a very patriotic red color and her eyes got huge. "H-hi."

Alex cocked his head. "You seem surprised to see me."

"Oh no. No no. Not surprised really, just . . . um . . . I mean . . ."

Dawn squeezed my arm. I know she was thinking the same thing I was: that we were about to be found out. I could feel the energy building up inside me again.

"I'm sorry. I mailed my RSVP late. It probably didn't arrive yet," Alex said. "Is it still okay if I'm here?"

I held my breath.

"Of course," Lily said. And she smiled at him — a big, beautiful, Lily-rific smile.

"It's good to see you," Alex said.

I'm lousy with time, so I have no idea how long they stood there looking at each other, but it felt like four-score and seven years. Or at least an hour. Then Burton made a loud sniffling sound, and it seemed like Lily burst out of a trance.

"You know Burton, right?" she said, putting a hand on Burton's arm.

"Burton." Alex nodded at him.

"Hi," Burton said, and sniffed a couple more times.

Another moment passed. But unlike the previous one, when Lily and Alex were lost in each other's eyes, this one was long in a squeamish kind of way. I thought I was going to have to turn cartwheels right there in the foyer.

Just then, Aunt Jane walked up and stood right between Alex and Burton. "Dinner is about to be served," she said. "Hello, Alex. May I escort you to your seat?"

"Thank you, Jane." He offered his elbow, and Aunt Jane took it with a grin. "It's good to see you back in town."

"Man," Bree whispered to me as we all headed into the main dining room. "I totally get why you guys are rooting for him."

"Yep," I said. "He's nice and funny and he loves Presidential Trivia."

It took forever to find our places. Dawn, Darby, and I were sitting in the back with Bree and some seven-year-old boy who was playing a handheld game.

"Great. Why do I have to sit at the kid table? I'm older than Mavis," Bree grumbled. She narrowed her eyes at the head table, where Mavis and Felicia were sitting, along with Mrs. Caldwell, Lily, Burton, Mom, Dad, and Aunt Jane.

"Aw, man, why didn't Aunt Jane let Alex sit with us?" Dawn said.

"Because she sat him where he and Lily could see each other," Darby pointed out.

She was right. Aunt Jane had placed him right up near the front, in clear view of Lily. Lily seemed to be aware of this because she rarely looked straight ahead, which was right toward Alex. And when she did, she turned the color of a strawberry.

Come to find out, the boy at our table was supposed to have been the ring bearer, but Mrs. Caldwell fired him because she thought his style of walking was too dangerous for carrying fine jewelry. "I don't care," he said, concentrating on his game. "Weddings are boring."

"You did the right thing," Dawn said. "The ring looks like a toilet seat anyway."

At this, the fired ring bearer looked kind of interested, but when he found out the ring was toilet-seat shaped and not toilet-seat size, he went back to his game.

The waiter brought out our dinner — a gooey-looking gray-colored loaf with orange sauce on top, a whole pile of steamed asparagus and carrots, and a little bowl of mixed berries — but even though it tasted okay, I couldn't really eat it. I was too busy focusing on Lily and Alex. Plus, all the trapped squirminess inside me was interfering with my appetite.

"But where's the food?" Mrs. Caldwell kept asking this one poor waiter, loud enough for us and pretty much everyone else to hear. "This can't be all the food. The newspaper is coming and we've got to be eating real food!"

My nerves were so jangly, I couldn't even stay sitting anymore. I bounced higher and higher in my chair until I ended up standing.

"What are you doing?" Dawn asked in a loud whisper.

"I need to do an emergency cartwheel!" I whisper-shouted back.

I started to head outside, but Dawn pulled me back down. "There's no time."

Sure enough, the lights were dimming. Our main plan was about to be set in motion. I wriggled in my seat as the music started up and the slide show came into view on the screen near the main table.

The first part was all Burton and the song about hero birds. Then came our part — the section on Lily.

We opened with "You Are My Sunshine" — one of Lily's favorite songs. Then came the pictures. The first photo was one of Lily as a baby, followed by Lily as a two-year-old, a four-year-old, and a pigtailed six-year-old. In each picture, she was all round-eyed and beaming. People kept saying "awww." I saw Mom look over at Daddy, and they smiled at each other.

"Did you see that?" Dawn said, nodding toward Mom and Dad. Darby and I nodded. We had.

Next came a hilarious photo of ten-year-old Lily surrounded by three screaming babies. Everyone laughed — Daddy loudest of all. Several people glanced over at us. Darby started to duck under the table, but Dawn patted her arm very sweetly.

Lily covered her face when her seventh-grade yearbook photo came on the screen. I know she's embarrassed by the braces and crooked bangs, but she still looks adorable. Next came Lily in ninth grade, then tenth grade, and then . . .

Then came Lily and Alex, and Lily and Alex, and LilyandAlex. Going to homecoming, throwing a Frisbee with us, going to prom, playing with Quincy, and just sitting side by side on the porch swing. In each one, Lily is smiling the way we never see her smile anymore — with her eyes bright and her cheeks pushed up and rounded, making her face all heart-shaped. That or her mouth is wide open in a laugh.

"Wow," said Bree beside me.

The Alex on the screen was dimpled and grinning, but the Alex in the room, watching the slide show, looked kind of sad. Lily was staring down at her plate. The whole room was hushed except for a distant twittery sound, which I soon realized was Mrs. Caldwell. She was over by Aunt Jane, trying to get her to turn off the projector.

Brisk movement caught my attention. I turned and saw Mom heading straight for us.

"Hoo boy," Dawn said. "We're in for it now."

"You will apologize to Lily, then you will apologize to Alex, and then Aunt Jane will drive you girls home. You will not be staying for the rest of the dinner." Mom's whisper was like the angry hiss of a venomous snake.

"Yes, ma'am," we said.

"Now!" she added and then walked over to Mrs. Caldwell.

"Oooh. You girls are in big trouble," said the fired ring bearer. But he sounded impressed, not mean. And it was the first time he'd set down his game since we saw him.

"Good luck," Bree said.

"Thanks," I said back. For someone who tries hard to look scary and tough, she really was pretty nice.

Daddy was already talking to Lily, so we decided to talk to Alex first. But when we looked over at his chair, it was empty.

"Oh no!" I said. I ran toward the foyer and collided with a tall man — only, it wasn't Alex. This man had a beard and mustache.

"Whoa there," he said. "You all right?"

"Uh-huh," I said impatiently, trying to peer around him into the foyer.

"Well, I'll be dogged. What's going on here?" the man asked, surveying the scene in the dining room. That's when I noticed that he was holding a camera. It was the newspaper reporter, come to cover the event. But instead of a proper dinner party, all he could see was a bunch of people gossiping, Mrs. Caldwell pitching a fit at the waiters, Mom and Aunt Jane comforting Lily, Dad comforting Darby (who'd crawled under the table), and the fired ring bearer with an asparagus spear up each nostril.

"Excuse me, sir," I said, and continued running after Alex.

I raced into the foyer, but by the time I made it to the door, Alex's car was already pulling onto the street.

"Is he gone?" Dawn asked, coming up behind me.

"Yep," I said, all forlorn. "Do you think he's mad?"

"Beats me," she said, pressing her nose against the glass door. "It might be worth it if our plan worked. Maybe now the wedding will finally be called off."

"I sure hope so," I said. "Because if it isn't, I'll probably be turning cartwheels forever."

CHAPTER TWENTY

Through the Perilous Fight

Dawn

Unfortunately, the wedding was not called off that night. Neither was the big lecture from Mom or the "I'm very disappointed in you girls" speech from Dad or the forty-five minutes of hiccups from Darby.

Aunt Jane did her best to defend us. "They were including photos from Lily's past. Alex is part of her past. No one told the girls to leave him out. Right?"

The worst part, though, was seeing Lily afterward. She looked . . . heartbroken. Her forehead was all criss-crossed and her voice was wobbly and she kept staring down at the floor. When we apologized to her before leaving the restaurant, she just nodded. She wouldn't even look us in the eyes.

Later that night, we piled up beside the swinging kitchen door and eavesdropped as Lily sat at the breakfast table, talking with Mom and Aunt Jane. This is what we heard:

Mom said, "Are you upset that Alex was there? Or that he left early?"

Lily said, "I don't know. Both maybe. But it doesn't matter. I've made my choice. I'm getting married tomorrow. I have to forget the past and move forward."

Then Aunt Jane said, "Hmmm. Well, now, if you were a history buff like your sisters, you'd know that it's important to move forward, but you should never forget the past."

And that's all we heard. Because then, Delaney got wiggly and knocked over a picture frame on the shelf nearby. Mom came out and gave us yet another lecture about privacy and sent us to the Triangular Office to sleep.

Only, we didn't sleep. Instead, I called a meeting to review the evening's events. Delaney got out a flashlight and we sat cross-legged on the floor between my and Darby's beds. We spoke in hushed voices and didn't dare turn on the computer, because if we got in trouble one more time that night, Mom would ground us till retirement age.

We discussed the slide show and how everyone reacted. We discussed how fragile Lily looked afterward. But most of all, we discussed that moment in the restaurant foyer when Lily and Alex were staring at each other.

"I'm telling you, they're still in love," Delaney said. "No matter what else happened, tonight was worth it because of that."

"But Lily isn't calling off the wedding. You heard her," Darby said. "Maybe we just need to accept things."

Darby's always surprising us with wild, harebrained stunts and schemes, but nothing shocked us more than what she'd just suggested.

"You don't mean —" I started.

"Yes, I do," Darby said. "I'm saying we should get used to the idea of Lily marrying Burton."

I shook my head. "But Alex —"

"Alex left," Darby said. "He didn't even finish eating his mock duck à l'orange."

"Is that what that was?" Delaney said. "I wondered."

"You'll see," I said to Darby. "Tomorrow, when Alex shows up at the wedding —"

"I don't think he's coming," Darby said.

I let out a grunting noise. I was frustrated with her attitude and fed up at being interrupted. "Sure he is."

"We don't know that for sure," Darby said.

"She's right," Delaney said. "What if he doesn't show up? What if he hates us now and never speaks to us again? What if we lose Lily and lose Alex, and Aunt Jane goes back to Boston and no one ever plays Presidential

Trivia with us ever again? What if the best days of our lives are over forever?"

I let out another, louder grunt, this time because I didn't really have any answers, and I really wasn't in the mood for one of Delaney's ramblings.

"Well?" Darby asked.

"Well what?" I said.

"What are we going to do?"

"How should I know? Why are you guys asking me?"

"Because you always have all the answers," Darby said, "or at least you think you do. And you're the one who called this meeting."

"So? That doesn't mean I'm supreme high commander. I just called a dang meeting. I thought we could exchange ideas, but you're the one saying we should give up."

"I'm giving you the facts as I see them. Just because you don't agree with me, that doesn't mean I'm wrong," Darby said.

"Well, you could still be a little more positive," Delaney said.

"Yeah, you're freaking out Delaney," I said.

"I'm not freaking out!" Delaney shouted.

"You are!" I shouted back.

"*Hic!*" went Darby.

I got to my feet. "All right! I called this meeting and now I'm going to end it! I'm tired of you two and all your whining. Meeting adjourned!"

"Fine!"

"*Hic!* Fine!"

Each of us stomped over to our own beds, and I switched off the lamp. I could hear Delaney crying and Darby hiccupping and crying. They'd want me to say they could hear me sniffling, too, but I wasn't. I just had a runny nose.

I hate it when we fight. Usually, if there's a misunderstanding between two of us, the third triplet helps settle it. It's rare that each of us is mad at the other two. It's awful, too. I always start out all clenched and blazing, but then, when I cool off, I feel like I'm getting smaller and emptier. I mean, I still know I'm right, but I don't care as much about convincing them. Being mad at my sisters is like being mad at my feet.

After a while, I heard Darby's shuddery voice in the dark. "I'm sorry I was a sourpuss," she said.

"I'm sorry I was freaking out," Delaney said.

"I'm sorry I didn't have any answers," I said. "Truce?"

"Truce," they replied.

Once we'd made up, it was like my mind started working better. "How about this?" I said. "Tomorrow, we'll call Alex and make sure he's coming to the wedding. If Lily can still go through with it with him sitting there in the audience, then we'll know we have to accept it."

We gathered at Darby's bed, put our hands together, and swore an oath to accept Burton as our new brother if Lily chose him over Alex. And we promised to never argue with each other again — or at least try real hard not to.

CHAPTER TWENTY-ONE

D-Day

Darby

The morning of the wedding, we woke up to some scary noises. They were sort of a cross between a moan and a growl, but we couldn't tell if they were coming from a wild animal or something supernatural.

Dawn and Delaney, being big sissies, voted for me to go investigate.

I followed the sounds down the stairs of the attic to the door of Mom's bathroom. It was open just a crack, and whatever was groaning was on the other side. My heart felt like a big gong inside me, and my arms and legs went all tingly — not because I was scared but because I was excited. I thought for sure I would finally meet the ghost!

I pushed open the door, and there, kneeling in front

of the toilet, was Lily. She was still wearing her pajamas, and her hair was in a messy ponytail.

"Lily?" I said.

She started to turn around, but then a shiver went through her and she leaned over the toilet and . . .

"*Gluuuuaaaaaaaugh!*"

The scary noise was Lily throwing up.

There are lots of reasons why we think the bathroom is haunted. For one, it's always chilly — even in the middle of summer. Then there's that strange knocking sound and the way the lights sometimes flicker. But also, sometimes, your voice will hit a certain note or pitch, and the whole room will buzz in this really loud, really creepy way.

Lily was hitting a lot of those notes right then.

"What's wrong?" I asked when she'd stopped and sat back. "Did Mom make creamed beef again?"

She made a little choking noise and shook her head. "No," she said kind of breathlessly. "Mom and Aunt Jane went to get tacos."

"But you love those. You always say you could eat potato-egg-cheese tacos every day for the rest of your life. You used to say you would marry them if you could."

She smiled weakly. "I still love them."

"Oh no — was it the fake duck? Did that make you sick?" I asked, worried that we might have unintentionally poisoned our sister.

"No no. This is just a bad case of nerves," she said. "Sorry if I woke you."

"It's okay." I sat with her until she seemed to be done and then gave her a wet cloth so she could clean her face.

"Oh, Darby. I'd hug you, but I'm gross."

"It's all right," I said, patting her on the shoulder. "Are you going to be okay?"

Lily pulled herself up to the sink. "Of course I am. This is going to be a great day — a wonderful, happy, special day," she said. Only she seemed to be talking to her reflection instead of me.

I went back upstairs and told Dawn and Delaney about it.

"Holy moly!" Delaney exclaimed. "That was Lily? I thought it was a riled-up zombie."

"It's time to put our plan into action," Dawn said.

For almost five years, we'd had Alex's phone number on a list of important contacts that Mom had stuck to the refrigerator. We sure hoped he hadn't changed it in the last few months.

I'm always too shy to call people on the phone, but Dawn and Delaney aren't. In fact, they bickered over who got to call Alex, so I intervened and said that Dawn should, since it had been her plan.

Delaney and I stood on either side of her — so close our three noses were almost touching.

"Alex? This is Dawn."

"Dawn?" we heard him say. "What's going on?"

"We just wanted to make sure you were coming to the wedding."

Alex heaved a long, staticky sigh. "I don't think so, Dawn. Last night was tough."

Delaney grabbed the phone from Dawn. "We're sorry!" she said. "We didn't mean to upset you. We were just . . . trying to show Lily's past."

"That's not what I mean," Alex said. "I mean . . . I just don't think I can watch her marry someone else."

Dawn, Delaney, and I made sad eyes at each other.

"But . . . but . . ." Delaney sputtered.

The next thing I knew, I was grabbing the phone from her. "Alex? You have to come. You just have to," I said.

"Why is that?" Alex asked.

"Because Lily is important to you. And even if you don't like it, you should support her in her decision — right? Isn't that what you told us?"

There was a long pause. For a moment, I thought we'd lost the connection. Then he said, "You girls are too smart for me. Do you know that?"

Delaney bounced on her toes, and Dawn gave me the thumbs-up. I felt pretty dang proud of myself, too.

"Okay, I'll come," Alex said. "But I'll probably be late. I didn't think I was going, so I promised a buddy I'd help him move."

Dawn grabbed the phone from me. "How late will you be?" she asked.

"I don't know. About a half hour," we heard Alex say. "I might miss the ceremony, but I'll be there for the reception."

"Fine. We'll see you then," Dawn said and hung up the phone.

"Fine?" Delaney asked. "But what about seeing if Lily could marry Burton while Alex is watching? We can't put that to the test if he's not there."

"Girls," Dawn said, putting an arm around each of us, "it's time for Operation Postpone, version 2.0."

CHAPTER TWENTY-TWO

Aide

Delaney

Our house was looking less and less like our home. Furniture in the living room had been moved to make room for two sections of chairs with a long white carpet runner in between. Fake white flowers were everywhere, including three white wicker baskets tied up with blue ribbons. They were on the mantel waiting for us to use them during the ceremony.

The wedding was scheduled for six o'clock and the guests were going to start arriving at five thirty. By five o'clock, people in the wedding were running around like long-tailed cats in a room full of rocking chairs. Everyone was busy dressing, arranging, and, in our case, plotting.

"Remember — divide and conquer," Dawn said as we stood in a corner of the living room.

"I always thought it was 'united we stand,' " I said.

Dawn rolled her eyes. "It is, but we'd agreed we could do more damage if we split up."

"*Shhhh!*" Darby held up her hands in a warning signal. Someone was coming through the front door beside us. To our surprise, the fired ring bearer walked in, wearing a tie and everything.

"What are you doing here?" Dawn asked.

"I changed my mind. Weddings are pretty exciting," he said. "Also, Mrs. Caldwell said it's bad luck to not have a ring bearer and that she'd give me thirty dollars if I do it right. I'm saving up for a new game, so . . ." He shrugged to show us how helpless a situation he was in.

"Well, good luck," I said, and we all shook his hand.

"Thanks." The rehired ring bearer hitched up his trousers, which were a little big on him, and headed for the sofa.

Dawn waited until he sat down and started playing his handheld game. Then she put one arm around me and her other arm around Darby and pulled us into a huddle.

"Okay. Everybody remember your stations?" she whispered. "I'm going to stall the preacher. Delaney, you stall the bridesmaids. Darby, you stay out here and monitor the guests as they arrive. See if you can make some mischief."

"What about Ms. Woolcott?" I asked. "Mom asked her to keep an eye on us while she and Aunt Jane help Lily get dressed."

We peered into the dining room, where Ms. Woolcott was sneaking refreshments off the buffet when she thought no one was looking.

"Greedy old bag," Dawn grumbled. "What kind of person shows up an hour early to a wedding? Especially when they live right next door."

"Give me your bow ties," Darby said. "I'll switch them out after a while so she thinks she's seeing all three of us."

I was more than happy to unclip my tie and hand it to Darby. I'd been wanting to yank that thing off since the minute Aunt Jane put it on me. The tie plus buttoning the shirt all the way to the top made it feel like a boa constrictor was hugging me around the neck.

"And take these." Dawn reached into the pockets of her trousers and pulled out our walkie-talkies. "That way we can keep in touch and send each other updates."

We waited until Ms. Woolcott was busy pilfering a stuffed mushroom and scattered. I went straight down the hall to Mom's bedroom, where the bridesmaids were primping.

"What are you doing in here?" Felicia was sitting at Mom's vanity, frowning at my reflection in the mirror in front of her. Mavis was also reflected. She glared at me from the end of the bed, where she was painting her nails the color of a tangerine.

Bree sat in the striped armchair by the window, flipping through a copy of *Southern Living*. She was already in her red dress and boots, but Mavis and Felicia had on full slips made out of shiny white material and trimmed with lace.

"I came to see if you needed anything," I said.

Mavis made a scoffing noise. "Aunt Edith told us not to speak with you — not after what y'all did last night."

"Aren't you speaking to me right now?" I said.

Mavis shrugged. "I don't always do what Aunt Edith says."

"Are you the one I talked to last night outside the restaurant? Or the one I talked to at the dress shop?" Bree asked, looking me up and down.

"I'm Delaney," I said. "The one from last night."

"How do you guys tell yourselves apart?" Mavis asked.

"Um . . ." I tugged on my collar, where the bow tie had been. "I always know who I am. And they always remember who they are."

"That was a stupid question," Felicia said to Mavis.

"Be quiet," Mavis said back to her. "You asked Aunt Edith the same question last week."

"I did not."

"Yes, you did!"

As they continued bickering, Bree leaned forward and lowered her voice. "So what happened with that cute guy from last night? After the way he and your sister were looking at each other, I thought the wedding would get called off. But here we are."

"It's still on, but we're hoping that —" I stopped, wondering if I should reveal anything. After all, she was Burton's cousin.

"Don't worry. I'm on your side. I don't hate my cousin or anything, but let's face it. He's already married to his studies."

My mouth fell open in surprise. "Wow," I said. "You read my mind, just like we triplets sometimes do with each other."

Bree looked proud.

"Okay," I said, making my voice real quiet. "Here's the thing: We need to stall the wedding for at least half an hour so Alex can get here in time. He's the only one who can maybe stop it."

"Cool!" she said. "What are you guys going to do?"

I glanced over at Mavis and Felicia to make sure they weren't watching us, but they were too busy arguing over whose hair was frizzier. Then I sat on the arm of the chair and whispered my plan to Bree. I told her about "divide and conquer" and getting assigned the bridesmaids — and the secret weapon I'd already set up that morning to stall them.

"Awesome," she said once I'd finished. "That's so crazy . . ."

". . . it just might work?"

"Exactly. So what now?" Bree asked. Her eyes were all twinkly like lights on a Christmas tree.

"I'm just waiting for a noise."

"What noise?"

"You'll know it when you hear it," I explained.

Sure enough, after a minute or two, Mom's bathroom started making those strange knocks.

Felicia gasped and Mavis jumped slightly.

Bree leaped to her feet. "Is that them?" she asked. She looked so upset, I was confused for a minute. Then she nudged me with the toe of her boot, and I realized she was just playing along.

"Is that who?" Mavis asked.

I tried to look like a nervous person who wants to appear innocent. "It's nothing to worry about. But we might want to keep it down."

Again we could hear bumps and rattles coming from the bathroom.

"What is that?" Felicia said, standing up from the vanity and turning toward the noises. "Is someone in there?"

"Not really," I said. "I mean . . . it isn't a human being."

"It's ghosts," Bree said.

"No way," Felicia said, even as she took a small step in the opposite direction of the bathroom.

"Everyone in the family knows this place is haunted," Bree said. She turned and scowled at me. "Why don't you just admit it?"

I made my face go saggy and guilty-looking. "They're not that bad. They don't hurt you or anything. They just . . . grab your ankles, and sometimes they mess up your hair."

"You're lying," Felicia said, but her hands reached up and smoothed her hair down.

The knocking sounds came again. I've got to say, they seemed even louder and scarier than usual. It was like our ghost was in on the scheme.

"Stop it!" Mavis said. "I don't believe you, but stop it!"

"*Shhhh*," I said. "You don't want to make them mad."

"Those are just . . . the pipes," Felicia said, but she didn't sound totally sure. "I don't see anything wrong with this room."

"You can see them if you want — sort of," I said. "But I wouldn't advise it."

"See them? How?" Bree asked. Mavis nodded behind her.

"She's bluffing," Felicia said to Mavis. "Don't listen to any of her nonsense."

"Fine," I said. "If you don't want to see, don't go into the bathroom, close the door, turn out the light, and wave your arms around, saying, 'Come out, come out.' "

Felicia made a *ffffft!* sound and rolled her eyes. "That's the dumbest-sounding thing ever."

"Oh yeah? Then go do it," Bree said. "Or are you too scared?"

Felicia had the same look on her face that Dawn gets when she's on the diving board — sheer terror hiding behind a ho-hum expression. "Come on, Mavis," she said. "We'll show them they can't fool us."

Mavis didn't seem happy about being included. But between Felicia's urgings and Bree's challenging, pirate eyes, there was no way she could back out without being called a chicken.

"Just wave your arms and ask them to come out," I said as she set down her nail polish and joined up with her sister. "And be careful of your hair."

Felicia made another huffy noise and they headed into the bathroom.

"Think it'll work?" Bree asked as soon as the door clicked shut.

"I guess we'll see," I said.

CHAPTER TWENTY-THREE

Phil-ibuster

Dawn

I hung out on the front porch, waiting for Reverend Hoffmeyer to show up. Even though we don't go to church all that often, he knows who we are and he's always really nice. When Delaney was little and got stuck in a tree outside the public library, Reverend Hoffmeyer helped her down. When Darby was in the hospital after the watermelon-jumping incident, Reverend Hoffmeyer stopped by her room and talked to her. And once, when we had a lemonade stand out on the road, and Darby and Delaney got bored and left, Reverend Hoffmeyer bought five dollars' worth, and I got to keep all the money for myself.

When I saw his blue station wagon pull up and park, I started to get nervous and bounced in my cowboy boots a little. That was probably why he said, "Hi, Delaney," as he mounted the porch steps.

"I'm Dawn," I said.

"Sorry," he said. "How are you today, Dawn?"

"I'm okay. I'm a little anxious about the wedding, though."

He smiled and bent down a bit to look me in the eye. He tends to do that whenever he talks to us, and we appreciate it. I always get distracted by the neat rows of his slicked-back gray hair, and the tiny gap between his front teeth.

Reverend Hoffmeyer smiled wide, revealing the space. It was the perfect width for a dime or penny, and I started imagining myself inserting a small coin. "No need to be worried," he said. "Weddings are supposed to be happy occasions where people can relax and feel good about life."

I was going to say something back to him, but the second I opened my mouth, we heard bloodcurdling screams come from inside the house. The screams grew gradually louder and then Felicia and Mavis came running outside in their slips.

"Good heavens!" Reverend Hoffmeyer exclaimed.

Looked like Delaney's plan had worked. I bit the inside of my cheek to keep from laughing. Meanwhile,

Reverend Hoffmeyer just stood there, clutching his Bible. He seemed at a loss. I guess in all his years as a preacher, he'd never run across someone screeching in their underwear — at least, not at a wedding.

The girls ran all the way to Felicia's Jeep, hopped inside, and slammed the door.

"I should probably go talk to them," Reverend Hoffmeyer said — only, it came out sounding more like a question.

I figured that would be as good a way as any to delay the wedding. "I think you probably better," I said.

I watched him walk over to the car and knock on the passenger window. I then peered into the living room and saw Delaney and Bree talking to Mom, Aunt Jane, and Ms. Woolcott. I made eye contact with Delaney and she snuck me a fleeting grin. I gave her a thumbs-up.

A sputtering sound told me Dad was finally here. I turned back around and sure enough, there he was on his Vespa, wearing his tuxedo. He gave me a little wave as he parked it beside the ruined althea bush.

"Hey there, Dawn," he said, undoing his chin strap. "Do I have helmet hair?"

It was a joke, of course, since Dad doesn't have much hair at all anymore.

"Agent Firstborn? This is Agent Second-born. Do you read?" came a crackly voice from my walkie-talkie. It was Darby. It sounded like she was hollering right from my pocket.

"What's that?" Dad asked, coming up the steps.

I pulled it out and fumbled with it. The doggone volume must have been turned all the way up. But before I could do anything, Darby's voice came again. "Firstborn? Do you read? Is the preacher situation under control?"

"What preacher situation?" Dad asked.

"Um . . ." I said, turning off the receiver. "Well, it seems Felicity and Mavis got a little worked up, so Reverend Hoffmeyer is talking to them right now."

"Uh-huh. And what, exactly, got them all worked up? Did you girls have any part in it?"

"Gee, um . . ." I never wished I was Delaney so bad in my life. That girl can come up with answers in no time. Long, wandering answers that make you forget what you asked and sorry you even brought it up.

Daddy doesn't have much hair on the top of his head, but he does have big bushy eyebrows. I watched as they lifted high on his head in a look of utter suspicion. "Dawn? What are you three up to this time?"

"It's not that bad. Really."

"That answer does not make me feel better," he said. "Are you three up to more shenanigans?"

I stood silently for a few seconds longer, rummaging all around my brain for an explanation that would make sense and not add five more months of grounding to my sentence. But I couldn't. So I told him the truth.

"We're not trying to stop the wedding entirely," I said. "We just want to delay it."

"But why?"

I told him we thought Alex was still in love with Lily and that she was still in love with him. I told him how they stared at each other in the foyer the night before and how the air all around us got warm and sizzly as if we were inside a microwave. I told him that we figured if Lily could say "I do" to Burton with Alex sitting right there watching them, then we would know that she loved Burton and we would do our darnedest to be happy about it. And I told him that Alex decided to come and be here for her, but that he was going to be late.

"I see. So that's the reason for the walkie-talkies and the sneaking around?" he asked.

I nodded. "We just needed everything to run late. I mean, what's half an hour versus the rest of Lily's life?"

Dad plunked down on the porch swing and rested his elbows on his knees. I sat down beside him. He looked lost in thought, and a little sad. Also, I noticed his hair was bent slightly on the side of his head. He really did have helmet hair — only, I wasn't going to say so.

"Girls, girls, girls," he said, shaking his head. "You know, more than anything in the world, I just want you three to be happy. And I want Lily to be happy."

"I know," I mumbled, bracing myself for the lecture.

"And you know what? I've been thinking about this and . . . I don't think she's happy."

I gaped at him. "Neither do we."

"So count me in. I'll be Agent Baldie." He looked over at me and smiled.

"Wha-a-a?" It took a little while for my mind to put everything in order: We weren't in trouble with Daddy — we were in cahoots with him! He actually wanted to help.

"Look. Here comes the preacher now," Daddy said, getting to his feet. Reverend Hoffmeyer was walking back up the driveway. "Everything all right, Reverend? I heard there was a bit of a ruckus."

"Seems to be," the reverend replied. "The girls just got a little overexcited. They're going to take a few more moments to calm down and then go back inside to get dressed."

"That's good to hear. Thank you for speaking with them."

"My pleasure, Phil. So how are you doing on this blessed day?"

"Not too good, Reverend. Not too good. In fact" —
Daddy put his arm on the reverend's back and steered
him right off the porch — "do you think you and I
might take a walk and discuss some things?"

Reverend Hoffmeyer looked somewhat longingly at
the front door. "Er . . . sure. That would be fine."

"Good. I appreciate it."

The two of them headed down the walkway, past the
Vespa, and past the green Jeep that Mavis and Felicia
were sitting in. Daddy looked over his shoulder at me
and winked. Then I heard him say, "I think it started
when I was about eight years old. . . ."

I pulled out the walkie-talkie and pressed the TALK
button. "Second-born, do you read? You aren't going to
believe this. . . ."

CHAPTER TWENTY-FOUR

United We Stand

Darby

When Dawn radioed in to tell me about Dad, I at first thought the walkie-talkie was broken.

"Something's up with this thing," I said to her, banging on the receiver a couple of times. "It sounded like you said Dad was helping us."

"He is!" came Dawn's crackly voice. Then I looked out the dining room window and saw Dad meandering around our oak trees with Reverend Hoffmeyer, talking his ear off. It felt like a dream had come to life — like finding a dragon or bumping into Santa Claus.

Things seemed to be going well. Dawn and Delaney had been successful with their missions, but the wedding was still T minus seventeen minutes and we were out of plans. I knew from Dawn that Reverend Hoffmeyer had talked with Felicia and Mavis, and that they'd eventually come back inside. Dad can talk a blue streak — it's where Delaney gets it — but even he was bound to wear out after a while. I still wasn't sure if all the stuff we'd set in motion would delay the ceremony long enough for Alex to arrive in time. I figured I should do something — but what? There's a reason why I was appointed the lookout while my sisters delayed people. I just freeze up when it comes to talking to someone other than family or close friends.

Most of the normal wedding plans were falling into place. Burton and Mrs. Caldwell showed up. I have to say, Burton looked nice — a lot less like a long-nosed burrowing mammal than I've ever seen him. He and his mom greeted the guests, who were already starting to show up. Soon Mom joined them. And so did Ms. Woolcott, for some reason.

I stood against the wall between the living room and dining room, watching everything while feeling shy and helpless. The tables of food and fake greenery looked pretty, as did the rows of white wooden folding chairs in the living room. The violinist wasn't there yet, but someone had set the music player to classical, and soft piano music filled the air. It was beginning to look like a real wedding was going to happen there — and soon.

"Hey there, kiddo." Aunt Jane walked up beside me. She looked so . . . un-Aunt-Jane-like in her blue dress.

"Hey," I said. "How's Lily?"

Aunt Jane stared down the hall toward Lily's room. "Hard to say. She's very pale, and hasn't been talking much. I keep telling her she's rushing into things, so she's probably mad at me."

"Don't worry," I said, patting her arm. "Lily never stays mad for long."

"Any sign of Alex?" Aunt Jane glanced around the room.

"No," I said, making the word long and whiny.

"He'll come."

"But he might not get here in time. Or he might not come at all! He said he didn't think he could watch Lily marry someone else."

"He'll come."

"But how do you know?" My voice was all whimpery, the way Quincy's sometimes gets.

"That boy loves her," she said. "He'll be here for her. You'll see." Aunt Jane lifted a tiny blob of frosting off the wedding cake with her index finger and plopped it into her mouth. "Now, if you'll excuse me, I need to go help your mother before she feels outnumbered by Caldwells."

She gave me a pat on the back and then headed over to greet the guests with Mom and the others. People were starting to trickle into the room, and there was a gentle hum of conversation in the background.

It was eleven minutes to six, and I needed some way to stop guests from showing up — some sort of barrier between the house and the rest of the world. If only I could hit a switch and activate a force field that would prevent people from coming inside.

Suddenly, an idea hit me. I wasn't sure if it was a good one or not, but I really didn't have time to mull it over. I needed to be more action-oriented, like Dawn.

I went straight to the mud room, to the little electronic box by the back door — the one that controlled our new automatic sprinklers. I figured if I could program it to start spraying, that would keep guests far away. It was a little crazy, but it was also just right. After all, no one would want to get soaking wet in their nice clothes.

Only . . . the control panel wasn't all that easy to understand. There was a dial and some arrow buttons that pointed all different directions, and two rectangular keys that had no obvious purpose. I stood there for a moment, trying to make sense of it, and finally decided to press random buttons and see what happened.

"Darby?"

It was Mom. I must have been so focused on the control box that I hadn't seen her come in.

I figured I'd play it cool. "H-hi, Mom. You look beautiful." That part, at least, was true. She was wearing a simple blue dress, like Aunt Jane, except it was in a different shade of blue and was cut in a different style. "So how are you doing?" I folded my arms and leaned against the wall, trying to appear casual — as if I hung around in the corner of the utility room all the time.

"What are you doing?" Mom's gaze was like glue. I couldn't glance away, even though I wanted to real bad.

I squirmed a bit, trying to think of some reason other than the truth that would have me fiddling with the sprinkler system, but I couldn't come up with anything. (Not that it mattered, since I'm the lousiest liar in all of Texas.)

"Don't tell me," she said, crossing her arms across her chest. "You and your sisters are trying to delay the wedding."

There wasn't anything I could argue with in that statement, and anyway, she said not to tell her, so all I could do was hang my head guiltily. "Sorry," I said.

Mom let out a long sigh. "You aren't doing it right."

"Huh?"

"Reprogramming the sprinklers," she said. "Here. Let me." Mom edged past me and started hitting a couple of buttons on the control pad. "You girls never did like this new system, did you? You much preferred those old sprinklers that I had to drag around the yard." She turned the dial, pressed another button, and said, "There. All set."

Whoosh! I could hear the rushing sound through the pipes of our old house. Judging by the shouts of surprise emanating from the living room, the jets of water were spraying high in the front yard.

I stared at Mom. "But . . . why?" were the only words I could manage.

"You girls have a point. Lily needs more time to figure out if she's doing the right thing. If this helps her do that, then I'm all for it."

"Wow," I mumbled. First Dad and now Mom? If there was ever a day to search for buried treasure and four-leaf clovers, it was this one.

"But," she went on, her expression becoming stern, "this is the only thing I can do for you — understand? In a few minutes, I'm going to have to play the part of the shocked, embarrassed hostess and come right back to turn them off. I can't let Quincy out of his kennel, or get him riled up, or show him the pile of brush and flower petals we swept up after you crushed the bush. Can you girls take it from here?"

"Yes!" I said, nodding briskly. "I know exactly what to do!"

"Then go do it."

I looked at Mom for half a second longer, marveling at her. Sure, she had on her stern face, but her eyes held the same worry I could see in Dawn and Delaney's eyes — worry about Lily. "Thanks, Mom," I said, hugging her around the waist. Then I slipped out the back door.

The experts fixed it so that the water wouldn't spurt onto the house, but a fine spray still reached me, pushed by the breeze. It felt fantastic.

I ducked to stay out of sight of the bedroom windows and made my way to the side porch, where Quincy was being kept in his kennel for the duration of the wedding. As soon as he saw me, he let out a whimper and wagged his tail noisily against the side of the cage.

I undid the latch on the door. "Come on, Quincy," I whispered. "Let's play. . . ."

CHAPTER TWENTY-FIVE

New Deal

Delaney

Bree and I emerged from Mom's bedroom to see total pandemonium breaking out.

Apparently, Felicia and Mavis had finally gotten dressed, but the continued knocks and groans coming from Mom's bathroom made them uneasy. They decided to go and do their makeup in the air-conditioned safety of Felicia's car, but, sadly, they hit the edge of the front yard at the exact moment the sprinklers went off. They were now standing in the living room, crying about their hair and dresses and dripping water all over the place.

Dad and the preacher also got soaked, as did a few other unlucky guests — including the Neighbors. Mr. Neighbor joked, "I see why you like our sprinklers better."

Meanwhile, many other guests were trapped on the far side of the property, unable to get near the house. We later found out that the violinist had pulled into our drive, seen everyone racing about and shrieking, and ended up putting her car in reverse and heading back the way she'd come.

Quincy, our loyal golden Labrador, was at that point nothing even close to golden. He'd rolled in so much mud, he'd turned a dark, gooey brown. He's always happy to be wet and filthy, and he really enjoyed seeing everyone running around and yelling. Figuring they wanted to play, he romped about with them, tripping a couple of folks and getting muddy paw prints on some more. Then he followed someone inside the house and was galloping around the living room, shaking bits of mud everywhere. Apparently, he'd rolled in flowers, too, because Burton was sneezing like crazy.

The fired-but-now-rehired ring bearer was still practicing in the dining room under the watchful eye of Mrs. Caldwell. Nearby, Ms. Woolcott had sneaked one of the veggie sliders off of the tray, but before she could eat it, Quincy came bounding over to her and licked the ticklish part of her leg. Ms. Woolcott screamed and dropped the slider, which bounced in front of the ring bearer.

And that's when I finally understood how they got that name.

The rehired ring bearer apparently didn't see the slider, and when his foot hit it, he skated across the floor several inches and then fell onto his rear end. As he tried to break the fall, he threw back his arms, and the pillow he'd been holding flew up into the air — along with the toilet-shaped wedding ring, which landed with a *ploop!* inside the mounds of icing on top of the cake.

Mrs. Caldwell shrieked, "That's a family heirloom!" Pushing Ms. Woolcott out of the way, she dove forward and started digging through the cake with her hands.

"Well, I never!" Ms. Woolcott exclaimed. She glanced down at her skirt, which was spattered with mud and food. Then she marched toward the front door, stopping beside me to say, "I'm going home to change. I'll be expecting *someone*" — she raised her voice a little and looked back at Mrs. Caldwell, who was up to her elbows in cake — "to pay for my dry cleaning bill." As she stalked out of the house, we saw a tiny dollop of frosting fly into her hairdo.

"Whoa," Bree exclaimed.

"Yeah. Whoa," I echoed. For a while, we just stood there in awe of the destruction around us.

Eventually, Mom came in to apologize for the sprinklers, saying there had been a programming error and that it was all taken care of. She ordered Dawn to take Quincy back to his kennel, told Darby to fetch some rags for the floor, and then she went to help Mrs. Caldwell dig out the ring from the cake. Somehow in all of that, she overlooked me and Bree.

Everyone was bustling about, except the two of us. Suddenly, Bree leaned down and whispered, "Hey, look. It's the hunk."

Alex was walking through the door. He scanned the devastation around him and carefully made his way past the piles of wet rags, sobbing bridesmaids, flying bits of frosting, sneezing grooms, and Reverend Hoffmeyer squeezing water out of his robe.

"Excuse me," I said to Bree. I made my way to a corner and pulled out my walkie-talkie. "Agent Firstborn and Second-born, do you read? Third-born here. I repeat, do you read me?"

"Firstborn here," Dawn said.

"Second-born here" came Darby's voice.

"What are your positions?" I said into the speaker.

"I'm on the porch with Quincy," Dawn replied.

"In the linen closet," said Darby.

"Good. Sweetheart is in the house," I said. "Repeat: Sweetheart is in the house. Operation successful."

I heard Darby let out a whoop.

"Well, thank the stars," Dawn said.

It was such a relief to know we had pulled off Operation Postpone 2.0. Now everything was up to Lily and Alex. The chaos had been worth it.

I bounced over to where Alex was standing in the dining room. "Alex! Alex! Alex!" I sang out. "You're here!"

He was not smiling. "This is y'all's doing, isn't it?" he said. "What have you three been up to?"

I hunched my shoulders. "We just needed to buy some time. We knew you were going to be late, and we didn't want the wedding to happen without you."

Alex sighed and raked his fingers through his hair. "You know, I love that you're each so smart, but you multiply it by three and you get smart at epic levels." He motioned around the room. "*This* kind of epic."

I glanced around. It was kind of mind-blowing to see all we had accomplished.

"You girls need to be careful that you use your powers for good, especially if you want to become leaders of this nation. You know what they say about heads of state: 'With great power comes great responsibility.'"

"Actually, I think that's from Spider-Man," I said.

He didn't laugh.

"Don't be mad, Alex," I said. "We aren't going to let anything else go wrong, I promise. Now that you're here, we can have the wedding."

"No, we can't," said a voice from behind me.

I turned around and saw Aunt Jane standing there, looking worried.

"I can't find Lily," she said. "I've searched everywhere, but she seems to have disappeared."

"Are you girls behind this?" Alex asked me.

I shook my head. "No. I swear."

"Well, I better tell your mother and father." Aunt Jane started for the living room.

"Wait," I said and grabbed her arm. "Don't tell them yet. Please?"

"Delaney, do you know where Lily might be?" Aunt Jane asked.

I started to say something and then got quiet.

Alex narrowed his eyes at me. "You do know, don't you?"

I bit my lip, suddenly overtaken by an awful thought: What if we'd been wrong? All this time, we were trying to stop the wedding because we knew Burton was wrong for Lily. But was Alex right for her? Dawn, Darby, and I loved him — but did that mean they belonged together? The thought jarred me like . . . well, like several powerful jets of water spraying up from the ground all at once.

For some reason, I just couldn't tell him. We'd done everything up to that point, and it was time for *him* to do something — to prove he was worthy of our sister.

"I know where she is," I said, "but I'm not saying."

Alex looked baffled. "Why not?"

"Because you should know where she is — if you really know her and love her, that is."

Alex peered closely at me again, but this time, his features relaxed. He seemed to understand what I meant.

"Go on, Alex. Prove us right," I said. "Go get Lily."

CHAPTER TWENTY-SIX

Truce

Dawn

While Delaney was lucky and got to talk to Alex, I ended up talking to Burton.

Mom sent me out with Quincy to try to drag him back to his kennel. It took some doing. I got his leash on him, but then it was like trying to pull a small airplane into its hangar — an easily distracted, eager-to-play airplane.

I finally got him in there with the help of a tennis ball and two jerky treats. Of course he started whining the minute I closed the latch, so I sat next to him and said nice things about him so that he would settle down. It seemed to work. Plus, he found a big glob of frosting on his tail that he could lick up.

I poked my finger through the bars to stroke his

forehead and told him over and over that he was a good boy. But as he grew quiet, I could hear another noise. A loud honking sound.

I peeked around the corner of the wraparound porch and saw Burton. He was leaning against the wall, blowing his nose into a handkerchief.

"You all right?" I asked.

He nodded.

"Isn't the wedding about to start?"

He shook his head. "Mother is cleaning off the ring, and Mavis and Felicia are blow-drying themselves."

"Sorry everything is running late," I said.

He shrugged.

"You sure you're all right?"

Burton leaned forward and pressed his forehead against the porch post. He looked puny and deflated. "I've tried to make her happy," he mumbled.

Hoo boy, I thought. Sure, I'd asked if he was okay, but I didn't actually expect him to open up. Why couldn't I have been Delaney, who can talk to anyone at any time? Or Darby, who's always trying to understand how other people feel? I'm no good at helping people with their problems. And I'd rather get five booster shots than listen to a ninny like Burton.

"Well, you tried," I said. "I guess that's that." I

figured such a concise statement might wrap things up for him.

Unfortunately, all it did was make him open up more. "I tried everything," he said, his voice low and muffled. "I listened to her suggestions. I took her advice. I never complained."

I fought the urge to hop the railing and run into the trees. *I can do this,* I told myself. *It's not too different from Quincy. Just pat him on the head and tell him he's done good.*

"I guess you can do everything right, but still not be the right match for someone," I said. "Maybe you and Lily are just too different."

Burton swiveled his head to look at me. "Lily?" he said, seeming confused. "I'm talking about my mother."

"Oh." Obviously, I didn't know anything. So I decided to just keep quiet until something made sense.

"She told me this would be good for my career. I'm smart, you know. But I'm not that brilliant with people." He let out a wheezy chuckle. "I'd rather be at the library than at my own wedding. How pitiful is that?"

I thought about all the time he spent researching and the way he carried his papers like a baby. "It's just the way you are," I said. "Books are easier than people. People are tough."

"Lily's great with people, though," he went on. "Everyone loves her."

I had to agree that was true.

"She never treated me like an oddball. Even when we were growing up." He let go of the post and stepped back to blow his nose. "Anyway, Mom says if I go into academia or law, I need to get better around people. She said Lily would do that for me. She told me I shouldn't let her get away."

There was a crackling on my walkie-talkie, but I turned it off. I figured nothing could be as important as this. It was like . . . learning to read. You know how, in the beginning, all you see are letters and you have to look at all the parts and sound them out to figure out what they mean — but then, after a while, you don't even notice the letters and all you see are words?

Burton was becoming a word.

"So asking Lily to marry you was your mom's idea?" I said.

He nodded. "She's always known what's best for me. And she's right. I need to get better with people — especially if I want to teach at a university. But look at this wedding. It's a disaster."

"Yeah, well . . . that's not entirely your fault," I said. I was feeling guilty about the way we'd ruined things for him. I still didn't want him to marry Lily, but at the same time, he'd never done anything bad to us. He just wanted to be around Lily more — and who could blame him for that?

"Mother is so upset. Nothing is turning out the way she'd hoped."

The way *she'd* hoped?!

"Jiminy!" I shouted. "I'm sorry, Burton, but your mom needs to figure out that this isn't her wedding, it's yours. And anyway, she's the one who pushed you into it. It's not fair to make you do something you might not be ready for and then get mad at you if it doesn't work out."

Burton looked thoughtful. "You have a point."

I studied his face. There was something sort of sweet about Burton that I never saw before. I could kind of, almost, maybe see how Lily could like him.

"You know, I understand needing to get better with people, because I'm not real good at them either," I said. "But instead of getting married, why don't you find some good friends? Maybe a couple of people who like books and research and stuff, like you do. The best part is, you don't have to go through a big, crazy ceremony to get yourself a good pal."

Burton laughed. A real laugh-out-loud kind of laugh instead of one of his gaspy ones.

"See? You aren't bad with people," I said. "We had ourselves a good talk."

"Thanks," he said. "You know what? You aren't bad with people either."

CHAPTER TWENTY-SEVEN

State of the Union

Darby

Back inside, things were starting to calm down a little. Some people dropped off soggy gifts and left, others never came in at all, and the half-drowned folks who chose to stay were now toweled off and making jokes. Most of the cleanup fell to me — which I guess was justice since I'd come up with the sprinkler system plan. I was carrying another load of wet towels and rags to the utility room when I heard Delaney's buzzy voice come over the walkie-talkie again.

"Firstborn and Second-born, do you read?"

"Second-born here," I replied.

We waited a few seconds.

"Firstborn, do you read?" Delaney said again.

Again, there was no reply.

"Dagnabbit, Dawn!" Delaney's voice hissed and crackled.

"What's going on?" I asked.

"Sweetheart is missing," Delaney said.

"What? I thought Alex just got here."

"Wait. . . . That's right, Sweetheart is Alex. What's Lily's code name? Darling? Aw heck, never mind. What I'm trying to say is, Lily is missing."

"Where'd she go?"

"I think we all know where she went. Alex has gone to find her and I'm going to make sure he gets her."

"Well, that's good. Things need to get rolling soon. Mr. Maroney keeps showing his knee surgery scars, and Ms. Woolcott has eaten half the mini quiches. And if that ring bearer tells one more knock-knock joke, I'll —"

"We have to delay it just a little longer," Delaney interrupted. "Can you stall the wedding guests to buy Alex some time?"

"How on earth do you want me to do that? We've already done everything except start a fire."

There was a pause on the other end.

"Wait — you don't actually want me to start a fire, do you, Delaney?" I asked.

"We probably shouldn't," she said. "How about just make a speech?"

"*Me?*"

"Yeah."

"Uh-uh. I'm too shy."

"Well, you have to do something, and quick. I'm going off to check on Alex and Lily, and Dawn has gone radio silent. We're counting on you, Darby. Over and out."

"But . . . wait! Delaney? Third-born?" I kept pushing the TALK button and fiddling with the volume, but it was no use. Now they were both ignoring their walkie-talkies. "Shoot!"

I pocketed my receiver and headed back into the living room. Delaney was right. Everyone was getting restless. People of all different levels of sogginess were squirming in their chairs, checking their watches, and glancing hopefully around the room. If something official didn't happen soon, people would ask questions. Then the Caldwells would find out Lily was missing and start searching for her. We needed to give Lily and Alex as much time as we could.

But why did it have to be up to me?

"Maybe it doesn't!" I said to myself. I scanned the vicinity for a worthy candidate. Mom and Dad were still trying to help Reverend Hoffmeyer get dried off for the ceremony. The rehired ring bearer was sneaking bits of ruined wedding cake while Bree tried to clean up the mess. Mavis and Felicia were in the kitchen retouching their makeup.

And then . . . Aunt Jane started to walk past, on her way to the kitchen with some of Mom's face powder.

"Aunt Jane!" I cried out.

She stopped in her tracks and looked over at me. "What's up?"

"Could you do something for me?"

Aunt Jane walked over. "Just name it," she said, pushing a loose strand of hair out of my face. "You know I'd do anything for you girls."

"Anything?"

"Hey, I'm in a dress, aren't I?" she said with a chuckle. "So what do you need?"

I looked at Aunt Jane in her purplish-blue dress with the shiny buttons. I could tell by the way she moved and kept pulling on the sleeves and collar that she was uncomfortable in it — but she wore it anyway. She never wears dresses. She hates dresses. And yet, she wore one for Lily.

Suddenly, I knew what I needed to do.

"I want to say a few things to the guests. Could you get their attention?" I asked.

Aunt Jane grinned. "Can do." She walked to the far end of the living room and stood facing the guests. "All right, everyone. Listen up! My niece Darby would like to say a few words."

Everyone fell silent. Aunt Jane beckoned me with the hand not holding powder, and people turned in their chairs to watch me approach. My legs felt all noodly and I was amazed to see my feet moving. It was as if someone else were controlling them.

I reached the front and turned toward the audience. *You're doing this for Lily,* I told myself. *And Alex. And True Love.*

The guests all leaned forward at once. Some folks were smiling at me; others just seemed baffled. Mom, Dad, and Reverend Hoffmeyer were among the confused-looking ones.

"I'd like —" I began. My voice came out all squawky. I cleared my throat and tried again. "I'd like to tell you about my family. A lot of you know us and you know that we're not perfect. I mean, what family is? But I guess we aren't real good at pretending to be perfect the way other families are."

A couple of people chuckled. Across the room, I could see Mavis and Felicia, and even Mrs. Caldwell, come out of the kitchen to listen.

"My mom works hard," I went on. "A lot of you know that because she does your books for you. If she doesn't and you're looking for someone, you really should consider her. Anyway, it's not easy to run a business and take care of four girls, a dog, and a house. But she does it."

Mom's mouth curled into a slight grin, and her face turned a rosy shade.

"My dad's a great guy, too. He's funny and loves to play crazy games, like I do. We don't see him as much as we used to since he moved out, and we miss him. But it's also kind of nice having just Dad time. Before he left, we saw him more, but it wasn't like we were always doing stuff together. Now when we visit, we talk and play games and joke around the whole time. So it's still good, but in a different way."

It was Dad's turn to look a little embarrassed, but happy, too. He and Mom kept looking at each other, shaking their heads, and smiling.

"Then there are my sisters," I said. "They are something else. Dawn always has the best ideas. Delaney has more energy than an electric-powered hummingbird. And Lily. Well, you all know Lily. That's why you're here. You know that Lily is like . . . the soft, sparkly light of morning. Like a breeze that smells like flowers when it's hot out. Or a cup of cocoa when it's cold."

I paused for breath. I couldn't believe I was actually up there, talking — and without hiccups either. All in all, it wasn't as bad as I thought it would be. And I started thinking maybe I'm not the shy triplet after all.

"Anyway," I went on, "Lily's about the best there is, and I'm really glad she's my sister. But I ask you to please keep in mind that Lily is entitled to make mistakes now and then. I mean, we all sometimes find ourselves doing the wrong thing, and —"

Right at that moment, the front door opened and Ms. Woolcott came bustling in. She was waving her arms excitedly.

"I just saw the most amazing sight," she said. "It's Lily! She's at the top of the hill in her white dress! And I can't tell for sure, but it looks like Alex is with her. With his arm around her!"

CHAPTER TWENTY-EIGHT

Independence

Delaney

Sure enough, Alex got it right. As soon as I told him to guess where Lily was, he hightailed it out the back door and started jogging toward the hill. I was bouncing on my toes, watching him through the window of the utility room, so happy he passed the test.

After I talked with Darby via the walkie-talkie, I slipped through the door to follow him. We'd worked so hard to arrange this moment, I needed to find out what happened. Plus, I wanted to make sure Lily was okay.

The thing was, I knew that if they saw me, they wouldn't be able to talk to each other — not in a real, opening-up kind of way. So if I wanted to hear them without being seen, I'd have to come up through the brushy part and stay very still. That's hard for me to do. Dawn and Darby are much better at eavesdropping than I am. Dawn especially. She can win staring contests with fish.

I cut across the yard to the part of the hill where cactus and cedar scrub are mixed in with the oak trees. The rest of the hill is cleared of brush and covered with wildflowers. Lily likes to sit at the top, lean against the oak trees, and watch the wind ripple the flowers.

It was hard not to race up to the top, but I knew if I did that, I would make too much noise. I had to be patient and carefully choose my steps to make sure I didn't break any branches or rustle any leaves. It was also a smart thing to do because of the cactus and rattlesnakes.

I poked my way up and knelt behind a big juniper bush. Lily had come into view long before I reached the crest. She was easy to spot because of the gigantic white dress.

Alex was just cresting the hill. He came to a stop a couple of feet away from Lily and stood there, looking at her. His arms were slightly out in front of him, as if he wanted to reach for her but wasn't sure if he should.

Lily's hands were over her face, and at first I assumed she didn't realize he was there. Then I heard her say, "Is everyone mad at me?"

"No. No one's mad at you. Your family is worried because they don't know where you are." He walked a little closer and sat down beside her. "What's wrong, Lily?"

Lily shook her head over and over. "I just can't go through with it. I realized a while back that I was making a mistake, but by then, it seemed too late. So many plans had already been made. So much money had been spent."

Alex's mouth curved into a sad sort of grin. "Just like you to not want to inconvenience people."

Lily let out a groan and put her hands over her face again. "Oh, I feel like such a fool!"

"You've got to tell your family. They love you; they'll understand."

"I know. It's just hard to disappoint them. And I don't want to hurt anybody."

Alex slowly lifted his hand and placed it, gently, on her shoulder. He patted her sort of stiffly and then Lily just seemed to slump over against him — as if her gravity gave out and sent her toppling sideways. Alex relaxed and put his arm around her. For a while,

no one talked and the two of them sat there, leaning into each other, the way I used to see them do all
the time.

I wanted to bounce around so bad, but that would
surely give me away. And if Alex and Lily knew I was
there, they would focus on me instead of each other. So
I pretended that a big, thick cement wall was going up
around the jumpy feelings inside me — damming them
up like a wild river. Amazingly, it seemed to work. Even
my toes didn't jiggle.

After a few quiet moments, I heard Lily say, "I'm so
sorry the girls got you mixed up in this."

"Hey, no apologies necessary," Alex said. "Last night,
I got to eat four delicious asparagus spears, and today I
got to see Reverend Hoffmeyer with a flowered towel on
his head. It was awesome."

Lily started laughing and then stopped herself.
"Seriously. I know how much they meddled. The girls
just never could accept that you've moved on."

"Who says I've moved on?"

She sat up and gave him a confused look.
"Haven't you?"

"Um, forgive me for pointing this out, but . . . you're
the one wearing a gigantic wedding dress. It seems to me
that you're the one who's moved on."

Lily glanced down at herself. "I guess I did. Even if I didn't want to."

"Wait. . . ." Alex scooted around to face her. "What are you saying?"

"Nothing," she said, shaking her head. "It doesn't matter."

"It *does* matter. It matters a lot. I don't know what happened last September. I've been trying to figure it out ever since."

"You wanted your space," Lily said with a shrug.

"No, I didn't. You suggested that we give each other space. I figured you wanted it, so I agreed."

"But I didn't want it. I just thought you did."

Alex's mouth hung open for a moment. "Seriously?" he said. "We broke up because we were being polite? Because neither one of us could admit what we really wanted? That's so . . . sad."

"I know."

The two of them were looking right at each other, so intensely, as if the rest of the world had dissolved and they were the only things left. Miraculously, my invisible dam held strong and I continued being still and quiet. But even if I'd charged out of the brush and started dancing around, I'm not sure they would have noticed.

"I miss you, Lily," he said.

"I miss you, too," she said.

Alex lifted her hand and held it between the two of his. I held my breath, waiting. And then . . .

Dawn's staticky voice filled the air. "Incoming! Incoming! Armadillo is headed your way!"

CHAPTER TWENTY-NINE

Mission Accomplished

Dawn

While Delaney was spying on Lily and Alex, I was still on the porch with Burton. We had no idea Lily had run off and were just passing time until the wedding started.

I think I'd just begun telling him all the reasons why he should vote in every election, when all of a sudden, Mrs. Caldwell came out of the house, shouting his name. "Burton! Where are you?"

In a flash, Burton was all upright and looking like his usual nervous self. "Over here," he called.

Mrs. Caldwell trotted around the corner of the porch and started waving her bony arm toward the horizon. "Lily is up there with that . . . that . . . Alex person. You need to march right up there and get her."

Burton rubbed his nose. "But the flowers . . ."

"Go and stop this humiliation at once!"

"Wait a second," I said, stepping in between them. "Alex is Lily's friend, and this is her house. She has a right to go sit up there if she wants."

Mrs. Caldwell gave me the meanest, most narrow-eyed, nostril-flaringest expression I'd ever seen in my life. "You are a child," she said. "And you will, once and for all, quit meddling in things that don't concern you."

"It doesn't stop you. You're out here telling Burton what to do."

"He's my son," she hissed.

"She's my sister," I hissed back.

"Enough!" She put up her hand and turned away from me. "Burton, go and get your bride."

"Burton, you're a grown-up. You don't have to do anything you don't want to do," I said.

Burton looked from her to me and back again. He also took a yearning glance at the road behind us.

Finally, he smiled at me, and for a second, I thought he'd come to his senses. Then he gave a defeated shrug, trudged down the steps, and began marching up the hill.

I ran after him, yanking my walkie-talkie out and shouting a warning to anyone who might be listening.

By the time we reached the top, Alex, Lily, and Delaney were waiting for us.

"You," Burton said, pointing at Alex. Then he sneezed.

"Burton, you shouldn't be up here," Lily said.

He turned and pointed at Lily. "You," he said, and sneezed again. But this time, it was three sneezes in a row. Something was wrong. His breath was too fast and a deep rattling sound was coming from his chest.

Burton shook his finger one last time at Alex, staggered sideways, and fell to the ground.

By now, the guests had filed out of the house, so everyone got to see Alex carrying Burton all the way down the hill. Lily followed behind in her big white dress, with Delaney and me skipping along beside her.

We could see Mrs. Caldwell pacing around and as soon as we reached the bottom of the hill, she started yelling at everyone. She accused Darby, Delaney, and me of interfering — which, to be fair, was true. She accused Alex of stealing the bride. She accused Lily of being ungrateful. And she told Burton that none of us were any good and that he needed to call off the wedding. Burton mumbled something that sounded like "No mo wehhing," which I guess was his way of ending it.

Meanwhile, the guests stood around and watched as if it were all a crazy play we were putting on for their enjoyment.

Mrs. Caldwell told Mavis and Felicia to gather their things and had Reverend Hoffmeyer and Mr. Neighbors help Burton to her car. After they got him buckled in the passenger seat, Lily stooped down beside him and said, "I'm sorry."

"It's okay," he said.

"It is *not* okay," Mrs. Caldwell said. "Young lady, I'll have you know that —"

"Didn't you say you were leaving?" Dad interrupted her. His polite smile couldn't hide the sternness in his voice.

Mrs. Caldwell lifted her chin. "Well," she said, turning to Mom, "I hope you're happy."

"Actually, yes. Yes, I am," Mom said. "Come on back inside, everyone. No reason to leave just yet. We'll enjoy the rest of the food."

So there ended up not being a wedding, but we celebrated love all the same — love of our family and friends and neighbors. Love of life and good food and our muddy dog. Aunt Jane started up a poker game at the dining room table, and Bree won most of the chips. Ms. Woolcott gave Lily a spray of real flowers from her garden, and Mrs. Neighbor even brought over some homemade peach ice cream. And Darby, Delaney, and I gave the rehired ring bearer ten dollars for helping us in our plotting — even if it hadn't been on purpose. Everyone was laughing and having a good time.

Mom and Dad had us explain all of our shenanigans to them, and we told them the truth — mostly. Luckily, they were in too good a mood to punish us. It was great to see them joking around with each other again.

Later, after we'd had our fill of canceled wedding food and had just poured ourselves some cherry-lemon punch, Darby asked, "Where's Lily?" We then noticed that Alex was missing, too.

The three of us went out to the backyard and, sure enough, there they were, silhouetted against the sunset at the top of our hill. Lily was resting her head on his shoulder.

"Think they would have gotten back together if this whole mess hadn't happened?" Delaney asked.

"I don't know," I said. "It sure seems like fate to me."

"Kismet," Darby said.

Delaney bounced on her toes. "I think I'd call it serendipity."

The three of us clinked punch glasses.

We're a great family. Divorce can't change that and neither can an almost-wedding. As Lincoln said, a house divided cannot stand, and I'd like to add that a house united can take on dang near anything.

ACKNOWLEDGMENTS

Deepest gratitude goes to David Levithan and Erin Black of Scholastic for sharing their vision and guiding me through this project. Like the Brewster triplets, we are an unstoppable team of three.

For her support, both moral and industry-related, my agent, Erin Murphy, deserves many thanks, hugs, and gooey desserts. I am blessed to be part of the magical EMLA team.

During the creation of this book, many wonderful people kept me focused, offered insight, and helped with the care and feeding of me and my family. Thank you to Gene Brenek, Shana Burg, Tim Crow, Carol Dawson, Clare Dunkle, Debbie Gonzales, Lisa Holden, Varian Johnson, April Lurie, Amanda North, Sean Petrie,

Margo Rabb, Beth Sample, and Cynthia and Greg Leitich Smith.

Much inspiration was drawn from my own eccentric yet loveable family, including Jim and Esther Ford, Amanda Ford, Jason Ford, Owen Ziegler, Sage Barton, and Fletcher Barton. Special thanks goes to my daughter and beta reader, Renée Ziegler, who gave invaluable feedback and was an early cheerleader of this story.

Finally, I give love and gratitude to Chris Barton, my critique partner and life partner, who married me during the creation of this book. Here's to many more sunsets in our Hill Country romance.

ABOUT THE AUTHOR

Like the Brewster triplets, **Jennifer Ziegler** is a native Texan and a lover of family, history, barbecue, and loyal dogs. Although she has only one sister, she does know what it is like to have four kids living in the same house. She is the author of several books for older readers, including *Sass & Serendipity* and *How Not to Be Popular*. Jennifer lives in Austin, Texas, with her husband, author Chris Barton, and their four children.